FICTION

INQUIRIES & ADVERTISING

ISSN: 2561-1933 (Print) 2561-1941 (Online)

Address: Suite 213, 3-35 Stone Church Road, Ancaster, Ontario, L9K 1S5

Advertising: Email info@mysteryweekly.com

Editor: Kerry Carter **Publisher:** Chuck Carter

Submissions: http://mysteryweekly.com/submit.asp

On The Cover: *Holmes*, by Christiane Ertmer, illustrator.

THE PASTICHE: A SHERLOCKIAN NECESSITY

Vincent W. Wright

Oh how I wish we had more Sherlock Holmes cases from the pen and desk of Arthur Conan Doyle. 60 just doesn't seem like enough. Like an incomplete story they leave more questions than answers. More problems than solutions. And more gaps in the whole picture.

The Canon has given us so much, though. Those cases that we do have seem to be timeless in their ability to attract new readers. But, we still want more. We need answers to questions about Holmes's family and Watson's military service. We want to read the unpublished cases that are mentioned, even the ones where Holmes didn't achieve the great resolutions to which we have become accustomed. We could discover more about the childhoods of our heroes. There could be enlightenment on the subject of Watson's marriage(s). More glimpses into the seedy underside of London would be at our fingertips. And perhaps we could finally figure out the precise location of 221b Baker Street.

Pastiche writers have been tackling these issues for more than half a century. They want answers, too, and since they can't find them in The Canon they come up with their own. These authors take up their pen and foolscap and do their best to fill in the gaps that still exist. They are not satisfied with just hearing about the singular affair of the aluminium crutch, or the giant rat of Sumatra—they need more. They need to put a story with the description so that their insatiable Sherlockian thirst can be slaked. Content to merely hear of a delicious event like the disappearance of Mr. James Phillimore they are not. A man doesn't simply walk back into his house to retrieve his umbrella and then disappear from the face of the earth. A hypothesis must be formed. A solution must be found. A new tale must be constructed to explain this away. It just has to be.

Doyle teases us with little omissions, making sure that even when we're done reading a story, we aren't done thinking about it. While we sit back in our favorite chair and savor finishing a tale like *A Study in Scarlet*, there's a little something in our brains which makes us pick up our copy of *The Complete Sherlock Holmes* and read more, since doing so might help alleviate the itch that was created by the author leaving out pertinent details. Maybe we would find out when Holmes first experimented with cocaine. Perhaps there would be some small trifle we missed before, such as more information about the one-time appearance of Holmes's housekeeper Mrs. Turner in 'A Scandal in Bohemia' and who she might be. Answers to these minor issues aren't necessary, but our love of the people and places in those pages makes it seem so.

I know several folks who are just as interested in pastiches and parodies as they are the original cases. For them, they are just as enjoyable. I myself have contributed to the literature of the subject with the three short stories I have written, and I am proud to be a part of the ever-growing body of work. I'm not sure, however, that my works provided light upon any of the botherations I have discussed here, and I didn't tackle any of the unpublished cases that are spoken about in The Canon. I did try and stay as true to Holmes and Watson and their environment as possible, and while I'm certain I did that, I don't believe my pieces will ever be considered great (or even close to great). They were fun to write, but they took me months because I pored over every detail and word in the hopes of not making some egregious error. Even after sending them to the publisher I wasn't sure they were done, and that's where having a good editor pays off. I do hope to write more in the future, I just have to do so around regular daily life. In time I'm sure it will happen.

Doyle, on the other hand, was able to put out new work at a rate which seems unbelievable to me. When you consider that he was a husband, a father, a sportsman, a world traveler, a political campaigner, a spiritualist, a Freemason, and a physician (among many other things), his prodigious output is almost staggering. And the works we have are the product of edits, rewrites, and numerous drafts—and all of it in longhand! I was truly floored by his bibliography when I discovered the extent of it. Having spent so much time as a student of only one of his creations was my sin. I had never perused another piece by Doyle until the summer of my 46th year of life, and now I am so sorry for that. It's all new to me, and everything I've read has given me that warm and comfortable feeling that only two other authors have. I am absolutely thrilled by the huge library of writings that is in my future.

If one is interested, it is possible to find Sherlockian pastiche from Doyle himself ... well, sort of. See, in 1896 he published a short story for a fundraiser at Edinburgh University. It was called 'The Field Bazaar' and is a breakfast scene involving Holmes, Watson, and a letter. It has never been accepted as part of The Canon of Sherlock Holmes, though. It's merely a fringe piece. A curiosity, if you will.

Two years later he published 'The Story of the Man with the Watches' and 'The Story of the Lost Special.' In these neither Holmes nor Watson is mentioned by name, but we do have the terms 'amateur reasoner' and 'amateur detective' to help us decide. (Unfortunately, nothing refers to Watson's presence at all). Here again we have stories that are debated as to whether they belong to The Canon or not. They weren't written, advertised, or sold as Holmes stories, and didn't appear in Holmes collections for many years.

These three pieces were written during the time of Holmes's death. Doyle had killed him off in 1893 so that he could work on other things. Yet it would appear that the detective and his biographer weren't far from his mind. These teasers were all the world had of them until 1902 when they were brought back in *The Hound of the Baskervilles* (which was touted as a "reminiscence of Sherlock Holmes" and not a return). To the delight of millions, though, Holmes and Watson were back in their chairs at Baker Street the year after that, and stayed there for the next quarter of a century.

In 1924, however, Doyle published a story that *did* mention both Holmes and Watson. 'How Watson Learned the Trick' was written for a special project called Queen Mary's Dollhouse, which was created to help show off British ingenuity and creativity. Several authors were asked to submit really short pieces to be featured in the book collection of the dollhouse, and at 503 words this one certainly qualifies. As with before, this was not written to be part of the Holmes world. It was a specialty item that was only to exist in one place. Holmes fans, though, couldn't let it go, and eventually it, and the others previously discussed, became part of what's known as The Apocrypha of Sherlock Holmes.

After the death of Arthur in 1930, his son Adrian took up the task of continuing the stories of Holmes. He enlisted some of the best writers of the age, and those publications have become legendary. People like John Dickson Carr, Peter Lovesey, Edward D. Hoch, John Gardner, and Stephen King have made their marks on the pastichean (new word?) world. Even John Lennon wrote one in 1965 with 'The Singularge Experience of Miss Anne Duffield.' Technically his piece falls under the heading of parody, but it's still a good way to get fans of a whole other artistic genre to read some Holmes.

The most common topic for authors, according to Philip K. Jones (one of the few authorities on Sherlockian pastiche), is Jack the Ripper. It's understandable, I guess—the world's greatest amateur sleuth was in full practice at the time that The Ripper was doing his deeds. Having both of them on opposite sides of the crime world, and with both being in London, people just can't *not* have Holmes tracking this guy. (Or woman, if you're open to alternative theories). The Canon says absolutely nothing about the case, so writers have taken up the charge of fixing that problem. I don't recall how many pastiches Mr. Jones counted that were about the two going head-to-head, but I recall that it was a substantial chunk of his listings of 10,000+ cases. This is a pairing that is not likely to go away any time soon. New evidence, suspects, and details about the Ripper case are found pretty regularly, ensuring that our interest will never fade. Add that to the ever-present popularity of Holmes and we are guaranteed more additions to this sub-genre.

My main area of interest in the world of Sherlockiana is the chronological side of the hobby, and thus I can tell you that things that appeared in the stories *can* cause problems with dating. Though not technically anachronisms, perhaps a word, phrase, or place is mentioned by Watson that may not have existed at the time when chronologists say the case has to fall. This is dismissed, or regarded, as the fault of editing. Maybe when "Watson" was putting the story to paper for publication it was many years later, and he might accidentally throw in an address or term that wasn't around at the time he wants the case set in. This is where scholarship comes into play. Since the 1920s readers have been tackling canonical problems with research. Instead of crafting a story to explain away these snags, they set out to solve them by means of information. The number of works done in this cause is so vast that it is likely beyond the ability of even the most ardent Holmes aficionado to grasp. Every subject in The Canon has been examined and re-examined for nearly a century, and this pathway can lead in many directions. Train schedules, weather reports, street numbering, Underground stations, types of carriages, telephone and/or gas line installation, historical figures … you name it, and someone has gone after it. But, not everyone chooses this way to resolve the issues. The pastiche writer decides instead to add to the existing literature. In order to do this, however, they still have to do their homework. Details have to be correct, so a study of the things mentioned in their piece is necessary. It's a wonderful crossover between the two different art forms, and to the loyal Holmes reader it adds a lot of credence.

But, no matter how much you investigate, and regardless of the cleverness of your plot, there is one facet of pastiche writing that will make or break your accomplishment ...

The voice.

One has to do their very best to get the voice of Watson (Doyle) down pat. To have the flow, the cadence or pacing, and the structure is a gift I believe only a few possess. I have read a lot of pastiches, and have come across precious few that I thought got this part right. Before I started writing my first one, I took a copy of The Canon with me to lunch and made notes about how the sentences were constructed, and what kind of terminology the major players used. I looked at descriptions, paragraph length, and the usage of senses to set a scene ... and I still don't think I got it right. I worked and sweated for months to get the wording just right, making thousands of changes along the way. They didn't even feel like drafts—more like complete rewrites each time. Still, it was fun, and very challenging. If one wishes to try something new that is technically tough, this is it. Somehow, though, many people make it work.

In closing, I salute the pastiche writers. They fall into a slightly different category than the parody and fanfic crowds, as they have to worry about their exactness and absolute obedience to the original Holmes books. The other media give you a bit more freedom, not that I'm discounting them in any way. So, I say, bravo to those who take up the proverbial pen and go headfirst into this amazing world. Yours is an intimidating yet rewarding task, and I am always impressed and thrilled when I read a piece that makes me feel like I'm holding a missing section of The Canon in my hand. It lets me know that the world of Holmes and Watson is still vibrant and alive, and that there exists still those who will never let it die.

THE ADVENTURE OF THE LYCEUM THEATRE CURSE

Michael Mallory

For every puzzling matter that has been untangled by my friend and colleague, Mr. Sherlock Holmes, there have been many more propositions for which he has refused participation. For those instances in which a prospective client's problem has been dismissed as lacking in intellectual challenge, or when Holmes intuits the person consulting him is not presenting the full truth of the matter, it has fallen to me to employ the so-called "bedside manner" of my profession to help the troubled caller over their disappointment. Most of those who fail to engage Holmes in their cases have left Baker Street with a sense of understanding, though one or two have reacted with anger, most notably a relative of the victim in the notorious Pemberton murder case, which was made redundant after it was discovered that the killer, Pemberton himself, had died. But none has ever returned after being rejected, which is why, upon hearing a rap at the door, I was surprised to see a very large, familiar man wearing a dampened tweed suit and matching waistcoat, a full, auburn beard that could have used a bit more trimming.

"How are you, Dr. Watson?" Bram Stoker asked, thrusting forth his hand, which I shook. "The landlady let me in. I am here to see Mr. Holmes."

"I'm afraid he is not here," I told him. "He is out braving the bleakness on a quest to obtain a new Bradshaw. Our old one has been reduced to tatters through overuse. Is there something I can help you with?"

"No, it is he I must see. I have come to appeal that Mr. Holmes reconsider the case I set before him several weeks ago." His words were delivered with a light Irish brogue.

"I cannot offer you much hope on that score. But neither can I answer for him or predict what he will do. So if you would care to wait for him, you are welcome to."

Keeping his hat on his head, Stoker stepped inside and glanced at his watch. "I have but a short time to spare. If the guv'nor returns to the theatre and cannot find me, there'll be hell to pay." I understood *the guv'nor* to be the actor Henry Irving and the theatre in question was the Lyceum, for which Stoker served as business manager. It did not take the powers of Sherlock Holmes to deduce that Irving was a taskmaster of the most stringent sort. Stoker settled down in our guest chair, filling it, and glanced once more at his watch.

Stoker had consulted his timepiece four more times before I heard Holmes's impatient footstep on the stair. A moment later, he burst into the room. "I trust you have made our visitor comfortable, Watson," he said, tossing the new Bradshaw onto a table and shedding his damp greatcoat, hanging both it and his hat on the coat rack.

"How did you know we had a visitor without even bothering to look?" I enquired.

"Oh, really, it could not be more evident. It is raining outside, in case you had failed to notice, and there are faint traces of wet footprints on the stairway as well as a small pool outside the door." For the first time he turned to look at me, casting his glance down at my feet. "Had you been outside in the rain, you would have removed your wet shoes and left them outside the door, as has been your wont since Mrs. Hudson complained about the stains on her new rug. Since there are wet footprints on the steps but no shoes outside the door, we are hosting another." Holmes stopped suddenly and sniffed the air. "I detect the faint odour of casein paint." It was then that he spotted Bram Stoker, who had stood up to greet him.

"I must have brushed against a freshly painted set piece at the theatre, Mr. Holmes," Stoker said, extending his hand. "I am so used to the scent that I no longer notice it."

Holmes took his hand. "I am not unhappy to see you, Mr. Stoker, but the answer remains no. I will not be drawn into talk of a curse, even if it is to refute it."

The first time Stoker had come to us he had hoped to engage Holmes in a case involving the supposed curse that has long surrounded the play *Macbeth*, a production of which the Lyceum was presently mounting. The theatre's manager and leading actor, Henry Irving, rejected such notions, but others in the cast, including Ellen Terry, who was to play Lady Macbeth, were more disturbed by them. To placate Miss Terry, Stoker had asked Holmes to pretend to investigate the "curse" and pronounce it so much superstition. But recognizing that he was being sought out merely as a means to an end, Holmes declined.

"The situation has changed we last spoke, Mr. Holmes," Stoker said. "I beg you to hear me out."

"It will not hurt you to listen, Holmes," I said.

"Oh, very well," he sighed, dropping into his favourite chair. "Pray, tell me what has changed."

"For one thing," Stoker began, "it now appears that Miss Terry's reluctance to play the role of Lady Macbeth was less a matter of concern of the curse as concern that the guv'nor's interpretation of Macbeth, which is that of a double-dyed villain from the rise of the curtain, rather than a weak man who is coerced by evil forces around him. Such an interpretation diminishes the effectiveness of Lady Macbeth."

"I am not a theatre critic, Mr. Stoker," Holmes said. "He could play the role as a pantomime grande dame for all the difference it would make to me."

"Um, just so. But since rehearsals have begun, strange things have happened. A fire broke out backstage, damaging some of the scenery. Its cause is still undetermined. Not long after that the batten holding a backdrop broke loose from the flies and plummeted to the stage below. The fact that no one was standing close enough to be killed or maimed was mere happenstance. Then a trap door in the stage floor inexplicably opened during a blackout, and one of our actors nearly dropped through. Now there are rumblings amongst our cast that the guv'nor, through his approach, has somehow summoned up the spirit of Hecate herself."

Holmes got up and walked to the hearth, whose fire was beginning to die down, and rubbed his hands over the remaining heat. "And what do you think, Mr. Stoker?"

"I believe someone is using the earlier chatter about a curse to arrange these so-called accidents in an effort to prevent the play from opening."

"For what reason?"

"I do not know. What I do know is that nearly six-thousand pounds have been spent thus far to mount this production."

"Good lord," I uttered.

"With that kind of outlay, the failure of the play to open would be disastrous for the theatre. I appeal to you, Mr. Holmes, to please find out the person behind this dangerous business."

"Has your 'guv'nor' dispatched you to deliver such an appeal?"

"No, sir. Mr. Irving believes he can surmount any obstacle thrown his way purely through his own efforts. He would not approve of your presence."

"Then why should I accept this case only to be turned away once your employer learns of my presence?"

"I believe I have come up with a ruse to ensure that does not happen," Stoker said. "I propose that you join us in the capacity of a supernumerary."

"A what?" I asked.

"A rather exalted term for a stage player who fills out the background for crowd scenes," Holmes explained.

"I could bring you in to play a lord or a soldier, under which pretence you could secretly conduct your investigation," Stoker said.

"Holmes is not exactly an unknown presence in London," I said. "Would he not be recognized by Irving?"

"When the guv'nor is working on a new production, the world around him ceases to exist. He sees only the play. Since Mr. Holmes would be a part of the play, that is the only context in which the guv'nor would see him."

I looked over to Holmes, whose expression remained inscrutable. "You must admit, it is an intriguing suggestion," I said.

"Do you really think so?" Holmes asked.

"I do indeed."

"Then I suggest you do it."

"Me? Come now, I have no experience on the stage. I wouldn't know what to do. You are the one who perpetually turns up in disguise, pretending to be everything from a beggar to a fishwife."

"We shall do it together, then," Holmes replied, a sly smile breaking on his face. "Four eyes will be better than two."

Before I could protest any further, he had agreed to take the case, to the visible relief of Bram Stoker, and I found myself unwillingly being volunteered to make my professional stage debut in the company of no less than Henry Irving and Ellen Terry!

The next morning, as per our agreement with Stoker, Holmes and I arrived at the Lyceum Theatre. It was an imposing edifice with classic columns in front, facing Wellington Street. We did not use the public entrance, having been instructed to report instead to a door on Burleigh Street. Stoker was waiting for us inside. "Your punctuality is most appreciated," he said, sliding his watch back into his waistcoat pocket. "Please come in. I will bring you to the stage from the back. If anyone asks who you are, particularly the guv'nor, please use the names Harker and Westenra. Mr. Holmes, you are Harker."

"Is there a particular significance to those two names?" Holmes asked him.

"Not a whit, I simply pulled them out of the fog because the initials match your own," the Irishman replied.

After travelling through a series of corridors and hallways, none of which appeared to be leading anywhere except toward more corridors and hallways, we emerged into the cavernous theatre, which was a veritable hive of activity. People dashed to and fro across the stage and out into the house, underscored by the sound of nails being pounded and wood being sawn. The smell of paint permeated the air. For me it offered the sort of cacophonous chaos that one normally finds only on a battlefield, but Holmes—or I should say "Harker"—appeared to be studying every person who flitted past him. He then cast his gaze upwards to the rafters, where men moved around on catwalks high above the stage floor.

"I must attend to business now," Stoker told us. "You gentlemen are on your own for the nonce, though I trust you will report to me any information you unearth relating to the question at hand immediately upon discovery." Holmes nodded to him, and Stoker turned around and vanished into the tumult.

"How do we even begin?" I asked him, all but overwhelmed by my surroundings.

"By keeping our eyes open and ears unclogged."

I did my best to unclog my ears, and through the din I was able to hear the sounds of a piano. Moving towards the sound, I soon found myself standing close to the edge of the stage. In the pit below was an upright instrument upon which the broad figure of a man wearing luxurious side-whiskers and a monocle was pounding out a stately melody. I recognized him as the composer Sir Arthur Sullivan, who along with his partner, Gilbert, was often sketched in the popular press. Standing next to him was one of the most singular looking men I had ever encountered. He was tall, but slightly stooped, and whippet-thin; his disproportionately-large head possessed features so sharp they looked like they might have been pressed, like the crease on a pair of trousers. The man had an untamed mane of coarse grey hair that mostly covered his ears. His most remarkable features, however, were eyes. They were narrow, yet still exhibited a penetrating gaze. That gaze was focused on Sullivan, and he appeared to be dictating that he wanted the music to be played at a slower tempo, which the composer did, to the man's satisfaction. He began pacing back and forth to it, taking long, lugubrious steps, now looking more like a human marionette. After witnessing this spectacle for another minute or so I heard Holmes's voice say over my shoulder, "I see you have located the *guv'nor*."

"Holmes, you cannot mean that strange-looking figure is Henry Irving!"

"Our leader and unknowing employer, and you must become comfortable with referring to me as Harker."

"I shall try," I said, having difficulty accepting that the peculiarly-proportioned wraith before me was reputed to be one of England's greatest actors. What ultimately convinced me was the fact that the great Sullivan appeared to be accepting the criticism of what I assumed was his music with calm equanimity, strongly implying that the critic was an artiste of equal, if not greater, stature. Once Irving had finished with Sullivan, he began clapping his hands and calling for silence, which was almost immediately granted him by everyone in the theatre. "Where are my soldiers?" he called in a surprisingly reedy voice.

From every direction came men who, like us, ostensibly, had been drafted to portray background figures in the spectacle. Holmes and I joined them in assembling on stage. Some of the men wore rudimentary costumes and wielded swords, and not terribly well. One of them, in fact, nearly clouted me on the chin with an iron-gauntleted hand, which was inhibiting his control of his sword.

"You men are brave soldiers," Irving cried, "the bravest of the brave, the warriors of the king! Let me see it!"

The ragtag army attempted to stand straight and tall, with many of them failing.

"God's wounds," Irving moaned. "The lot of you could not vanquish the Green Park Women's Lawn Tennis Squad! Have any of you actually served in Her Majesty's army?"

"I have," I heard a voice say, and to my horror, realized it was my own, having responded without even thinking. As a result, Irving turned his pale gaze in my direction and loped up to me. "I have not seen you here before, have I?"

"I was just recruited by Mr. Stoker."

"Ah, yes, Mr. Stoker," he said, almost dismissively. "What is your name?"

"John Wat ..." I stopped, having nearly blurted out my real name. "Westenra, sir. John Westenra. Formerly with the Fifth Northumberland Fusiliers, in Afghanistan."

"Well, Fusilier Westenra, you have just been promoted to Captain of King Duncan's Royal Scots Legion." He swept his arm dramatically over the collection of men. "This is your army. Get them to looking and acting as soldiers, and God go with you." He turned away, leaving me to command the men, some of whom were far too old to be genuine soldiers. A few appeared to be on the verge of falling asleep.

"Very well, chaps," I said, straining to achieve a note of authority, "we shall begin by coming to attention." No one moved. Finally one man, a thin-faced scarecrow in excess of sixty years, shuffled forward. "Look, guv, we got nothin' 'gainst you," he began, "But we was here all last evenin'. We ain't been home. The guv'nor, he never stops, he never gets tired, least he never seems to. But the rest of us is too exhausted to stand upright." There was a general murmur of agreement through the aggregation of would-be soldiers.

"Come with me, men," I said, leading them back stage and down a staircase that led to the wardrobe areas. Once the weary unit had reassembled, I said, "Listen up, chaps. I will leave you here to rest as long as I am allowed to do so. If you are able to sleep through the noise above, go ahead. But make no commotion of any kind or else our little ruse will be discovered." There was a flurry of muttered thanks throughout the ranks. "All I ask," I went on, "is that when we return to the stage, you will endeavour to stand as erect and soldierly as you possibly can. You, sir ..." I pointed to the man who had spoken earlier.

"The name's Dobbins."

"Mr. Dobbins, I appoint you lieutenant and charge you with keeping the peace."

"That won't be a problem, cap'n."

I would have continued questioning Dobbins, in hopes of gleaning more information, but we were interrupted by sound of a loud shriek coming from above. "Is that part of the play?" I asked.

"Not a part I ever heard," Dobbins said.

I raced through the underground rooms and ran back up the staircase to find even greater confusion on stage than before. A moment later, another scream pierced the air. "That sounds like Ellen!" I heard Irving cry, and saw him racing toward the backstage area. Holmes was running just behind him, while a handful of stagehands followed. I joined the procession. A cry for help directed us to a point at the rear of the stage, where I saw a beautiful, pale, red-haired woman backed into the corner of the building, eyes-wide, staring down in front of her.

"Great God!" someone shouted, and the crowd of men started to back up. I broke through, as did Holmes and Irving, and saw that from which the actress was recoiling in horror: a huge, brown adder!

"Ellen!" Irving shouted. "Don't move!"

"I ... could not ... if I so wished ..." she whispered.

What only moments before had been a hive of activity now transformed into a wax museum exhibit, with only the adder, which was less than two feet in front of Miss Terry, demonstrating movement. As we watched with horror, it raised its head menacingly in front of her.

"We must do something!" I cried.

With a rapid movement, a lean, dark-haired man leapt to a nearby property table upon which rested a sword, grabbed it, and in one smooth lunge plunged the tip of the blade through the neck of the snake. The creature coiled frantically, and then fell limp. So, nearly, did Ellen Terry.

Irving rushed to her side to comfort her. Then he turned to the man who had dispatched the snake and said, "We are all indebted to you, Mr. Naismith. I would like to retract my earlier criticisms of your performance as Banquo."

"Take me out front, Henry," Miss Terry uttered. "I need to sit down."

"Mr. Naismith, would you further do me the service of escorting Miss Terry to the orchestra?"

"Of course," the actor said, practically carrying the frightened actress across the stage, down the stairs, and into a row seat. As he was doing so, Irving called for the assembled cast and crew to gather around him.

"Clearly someone has been careless in leaving open a door or window and allowing a snake to enter the theatre," he charged. "As a result, Miss Terry has had a great shock. I demand that everyone be more careful about their comings and goings to and from the theatre. If I wish a snake to enter the Lyceum, I shall invite the critic myself."

His witticism was accepted with a round of laughter, which effectively broke the tension.

"Seriously, my friends, I entreat you to make certain no doors are left open behind you."

Bram Stoker now appeared in the house, lumbering his way toward the stage. "What's happened?" he asked.

"Come and see for yourself," Irving said sharply, leading him backstage. Holmes and I followed at a distance. "Ellen was frightened nearly to death by this."

"Good God!" Stoker cried upon seeing the dead snake. "Where did that thing come from?"

"I suspect it came over from Covent Garden Market through a carelessly opened door," Irving said.

"They sell snakes now at the market?" Stoker asked, innocently.

"For God's sake, Bram, stop being such a dolt! They sell *food* at the market, and wherever there is food, there are rodents, and wherever there are rodents, there are creatures that feed upon rodents, such as that brown nightmare. Somehow, it made its way from the market to here, and into the theatre."

"Has this ever happened before?" Holmes asked.

Irving turned his gaze upon him. "Who are you, sir?"

"My name is Harker," Holmes told him. "I have been engaged as a supernumerary."

"Another of Mr. Stoker's recent charges, eh? Well, get back to whatever it was you were doing. Bram, would you be so good as to make use of your heritage and drive this snake out of my theatre." Irving loped across the stage and down to the orchestra, where Ellen Terry remained seated.

"Saint Patrick help us," Stoker muttered when he was gone. "It's a miracle that thing did not strike Miss Terry."

"There was little chance of that, actually," Holmes said. "Intimidating though they appear, and venomous though they are, *vipera berus* are not particularly aggressive toward people. They strike only defensively, or, in the case of females, if they are carrying their young. It is too late in the year for that, which means its striking defensively would have required Miss Terry to try and touch it or pick it up, which I do not believe she would have attempted. No, its purpose was to instil fear, not serve as a means of murder."

Stoker pulled out a handkerchief and tentatively picked up the carcass of the snake. He carried it to a door at the very back of the stage and tossed it out, and then returned. "Things are getting out of hand, I fear," he said. "You must get to the bottom of this, Mr. Holmes, and quickly."

Once he had gone, Holmes said, "Watson, there is more danger here than even our Irish friend suspects."

"I thought you said the snake would not have struck unless it had been handled."

"Precisely. The very fact that it was here meant that someone had to handle it in order to get it inside the theatre. That implies that our malefactor is willing to take immense risks to play this grim game. Perhaps deadly risks."

Irving's voice was heard again, calling for the attention of everyone present, and thin though it was, it filled the theatre. "Even though I feel we can ill afford it," he began, "I must perforce call off rehearsal for the day, until Miss Terry fully recovers. You are all excused, though please be here at eight on the dot tomorrow morning."

"Perhaps we should stay and continue investigating," I whispered to Holmes.

"Our continued presence would be suspicious," he said. "Since we have been released for the day, we would do best to go."

It was shortly after ten o'clock that evening, after Holmes and I had supped, that Mrs. Hudson knocked on the door and announced we had visitors. To say I was startled to see the prim, high-hatted visage of Henry Irving standing in the hallway of 221b Baker Street, with a chastised-looking Bram Stoker behind him, is an understatement. "May we come in, *Mr. Westenra*," Irving asked, pronouncing my *nom de guerre* with dripping sarcasm.

"Um, yes, of course, sir," I said, ushering him inside.

"To what do we owe this pleasure?" Holmes asked.

"To the fact that my little scheme was for naught," Stoker admitted. "You were detected."

"A blind man could have seen that the two of you were not simply drafted off of the street for the ranks of the supernumeraries," Irving said, through a self-satisfied smirk. "I confronted Stoker, who finally told me who you were, and what he had put you up to. Gentlemen, if there is a problem in my theatre, it is my problem and not yours. In short, Mr. Holmes, I neither require your assistance, nor appreciate it's being foisted upon me." He gave a sharp side-glance to Stoker. "However, you, doctor, may still be of use to me, given your military experience."

"Mr. Irving, whether you appreciate it or not, there is a danger lurking within your theatre," Holmes said.

Glaring at him as though he were sizing him up for a hanging, the actor replied, "Sir, you are not going to try and convince me there actually is a curse upon *Macbeth*, are you?"

"Hardly. Your threat, as all threats, comes from very human hands."

"Who would wish to destroy my play? Or me?"

"I cannot say at present. But if I am to be dismissed, we shall never know, shall we?"

Irving placed a forefinger on the side of his nose and tapped it, as he appeared to lose himself in thought. Finally, he said: "Very well, you may return, Mr. Holmes. But adhere to your assigned position as a supernumerary. If you happen to detect something untoward, then you will immediately bring it to my attention. I expect to see you two on the morrow." With that, Irving made his way out, with Stoker trailing like a faithful dog.

The morrow came at its appointed time, though it was even greyer and wetter than the day before. Holmes and I arrived at the Lyceum at eight and took up our duties as best we could. Meanwhile, the chaos continued around us, with workmen fashioning the settings, costumers presenting designs for Irving's approval, and technicians working out the details of creating a storm on stage for the witches' scene, while actors milled about awaiting the approval of their director. Amidst the flurry of activity was Ellen Terry, appearing to be recovered from the incident with the snake. We worked until noon and then were allowed a brief break, a luxury in an Irving production, from what I had gleaned from my soldiers. I took the opportunity to compare notes with Holmes. "Given the sheer amount of people and activity happening all at once, it is hardly surprising that more accidents do not occur," I told him. "But I have discovered nothing pertinent."

"Nor have I," he replied. "At least nothing that appears pertinent to the matter at hand. It is almost as though the perpetrator of these 'accidents,' like Irving himself, has realized that I am on the case, and thus has decided not to chance another one."

"Holmes, you don't suppose that *Irving*—"

"I do not," he said. "I would sooner believe that Stoker is behind it, for reasons of generating publicity for the play, though neither supposition rings true to character."

After our break, the actors returned to begin rehearsing scenes on the stage, the technicians having been dismissed for the afternoon. "We shall begin with the feast scene," Irving announced. "My lords and nobles, please take your seats at the table." A group of actors did so. "Mr. Naismith, this is your big moment," Irving called, but Naismith, who had so efficiently dispatched the serpent yesterday, did not come forward. "Naismith, do not keep us waiting! This is the scene in which Banquo appears as the ghost that only Macbeth can see." After another long pause, sans the appearance of Mr. Naismith, Irving shouted: "Damnation, man, you clearly do not understand your role! You are supposed to appear to me, not disappear to me!" When the actor once more failed to materialize, Irving instructed that Stoker be fetched. Within seconds, the harried business manager appeared on stage. "We are all ready to proceed, Bram," he said, "but it appears we are lacking Mr. Naismith."

"I haven't seen him," Stoker replied.

"Well, *find* him, and be quick about it!"

With a resigned look, Stoker dashed backstage to begin his search. A few moments later, we heard a sharp cry, "Good God!" followed by: "Guv'nor, come quickly!"

Led by Irving, Holmes and I ran toward the voice, followed by a handful of others. We soon found ourselves at the opening of a spiral staircase that led to the level below. Stoker stood at the top of the staircase; at its bottom was the form of a man, sprawled out on the floor. Irving was the first to descend, leaping over the prone figure at the bottom, and turning him over. In the dim light I could see that his head lolled unnaturally as it turned. The hilt of a short sword was embedded into his stomach.

"My god, it is Naismith!" Irving cried.

Holmes rushed down the staircase and immediately began examining the body. "Wa … stenra," he called, "come quickly."

I dashed down the wrought-iron helix. One brief touch of the man's throat told me that that my professional services would not be required; Naismith was quite dead.

"It's the curse," a voice above us whispered.

"Stop that!" Irving ordered. "I will bear no such talk in my theatre! All of you, get back to your duties. We will handle this. Bram, fetch the police."

Without asking any questions, Stoker hastened away again.

"I recognize the handle of this sword," Irving went on. "It is one of our props. Even though the blade has been dulled, I imagine it could be deadly if one fell upon it."

"You believe that to be the case?" Holmes inquired.

"What else? Naismith was carrying the sword, slipped or tripped at the top of the staircase, and fell down it in such a way that he impaled himself on it. Most unfortunate. A tragic accident."

"Not to mention one which will necessitate recasting the role of Banquo," Holmes said.

"That should not be a problem. I was growing rather disenchanted with Mr. Naismith's performance in rehearsals anyway. For someone who claimed to have acted at the Memorial Theatre in Stratford, he seemed shockingly ill at ease with the verse." Then Irving looked up at Holmes. "What business is it to you that I must recast? Are you angling for the role? Would appearing in a Lyceum production enhance your professional résumé?"

Before Holmes could reply, Stoker's voice called from up above, "Henry, the constables are here."

"I must go up to speak to them," Irving muttered, "and I fear I must dismiss the company for the evening yet again. God's blood."

As Irving ascended the staircase to talk with the police, Holmes began examining the body of Naismith, paying particularly attention to the shoes the dead man was wearing. He withdrew when the constables came downstairs. Five minutes later, Inspector Gregson of Scotland Yard joined them. "Holmes, what are you doing here?" he asked. "What's this about?"

"Murder, Gregson. Cold blooded murder."

"That is not Mr. Irving's judgment."

"Mr. Irving's judgment is coloured by the footlights."

"Mm-hmm," the inspector drawled, ordering three officers to take charge of the body while he ascended the stairs to speak with the theatre manager. Meanwhile, the officers struggled to carry the remains of poor Naismith back up the staircase, a slow and clumsy process. Once they had taken the body out, Holmes and I ascended.

Looking down the staircase, I muttered, "Why are you convinced this was no accident, Holmes?"

"Putting aside the fact that the man knew how to handle a sword, something both of us witnessed first-hand with that business with the brown adder, this staircase is made of wrought iron and the treads of each step are rough, so as to prevent slipping. A man tumbling down such a staircase would show its effects either through rips in his clothing, due to contact with the metal edges, or scuffs on the tops of his shoes. The victim possessed neither, just as I predict he will show none of the heavy bruising that would accompany such a tumble. There is something else, as well."

"What's that?"

"Watson, do you trust me?"

"Of course I do, implicitly."

"It is your left shoulder that is the bad one, is it not?"

"The one that took the Jezail bullet, yes, though surprisingly, it is not bothering me at present. Often in weather such as this, it does. Why do you ask?"

"Look down there, quickly!" he cried, and immediately I redirected my attention to the bottom of the staircase. In the next instant I found myself all but flying headlong toward the iron steps of the staircase! Crying out, I reached my left hand to grasp the rail, while catching myself with my right on the third step. Thus I was able to prevent myself from tumbling down the dangerous stair. I was, however, in a state of intense ire.

"Damn it, Holmes, you *pushed* me!" I cried, balancing precariously upside-down on the stair. "What in heaven's name were you thinking?"

Reaching out, he grabbed my right arm and supported me until I was able to get my footing on the stair. "Watson, you have my most abject apologies," he said. "If, for a moment, I believed you were in serious danger of being injured, I would not have taken such a rash measure."

"Why did you then?" I demanded, climbing back to the top.

"To eliminate the last vestige of doubt in my conclusion that, given the shape and the narrowness of this staircase, it would be virtually impossible to fall the entire length of it without either becoming lodged, or grabbing onto something to stop yourself. Even with one shoulder weaker than the other, and with no warning whatsoever, you were able to protect yourself and prevent injury. There is no longer any question in my mind that Naismith was slain at the bottom of the stairs, after which his body was arranged to make it appear that he had fallen. I am confident that inspection of his body by the medical examiner will confirm that, as he will find no sign of bruising as would have resulted from a deadly tumble. I hope you will forgive me."

"I may, on the condition that should you wish to repeat this experiment for Gregson, we shall reverse places."

Holmes laughed and shook my hand with vigour, most likely because he understood there would be no way possible for me to surprise him in such manner. Having calmed myself somewhat, I asked him: "Why do you suppose the fellow had to die?"

"Ah, my friend, that is what we must discover. Since we have once more been released, I intend to spend the rest of my day at the British Library. Would you care to join me?"

"I had best return to Baker Street," I said, knowing that once Holmes ensconced himself there, only a flash fire inside the building would coerce him to leave again. It was, therefore, something of a surprise to see him back home by late afternoon. "Did you find what you were looking for?" I asked.

"I did, in the newspaper collection. It seems the critics were much more taken with the Shakespearean performances of Gabriel Naismith than was Henry Irving. In particular, his Gonzalo and his Polonius at the Memorial Theatre were universally praised."

"When you see Irving tomorrow, you should tell him so."

"Oh, I shall, Watson." This was said with a peculiar, and to me indecipherable, smile.

However, the next morning we returned to the Lyceum to find a sign posted at the staff entrance, proclaiming that rehearsals had been suspended indefinitely, pending the search for a replacement actor for the role of Banquo. "It would appear the curse has been more effective than I might have supposed," Holmes said. We had no choice but to return to Baker Street.

For four days we heard nothing from Stoker or Irving, during which time Holmes suffered from sullenness and nervous agitation. He even threatened to revert to his pernicious and dangerous habit of injecting a cocaine solution in order to alleviate his boredom. I knew it was the unresolved mystery of the murder of Gabriel Naismith that was preying upon his mind, but there was nothing I could do to help him. I was therefore most heartened and relieved when, on the evening of the 29th we were once more visited by Bram Stoker.

"I felt you should be apprised of the situation at the Lyceum," he began, clearly in a more convivial mood than he was the last time we saw him. "After a more prolonged down-time than anticipated, in part because talk of the 'curse' had started to make the rounds through the West End, complicating the search for a new actor, we have replaced Mr. Naismith with Mr. Niall Wentham. He is proving to have a better grasp on the role of Banquo than did his unfortunate predecessor, and rehearsals have begun anew. I am happy to state that not one mishap has occurred since the re-start of rehearsals. The guv'nor is happy, Miss Terry is happy, even the supernumeraries are splendidly martial, thanks to you, Dr. Watson. My purpose tonight is to thank you for your services, and settle the account. What do we owe you, Mr. Holmes?"

"The opportunity to return to the Lyceum," he said.

"Is something troubling you?"

"The very fact that the incidents which persuaded some to believe in a curse should end so abruptly is the matter troubling me."

"Really, Mr. Holmes, you surprise me, given your reputation," Stoker said.

"Indeed?"

"Yes. Isn't it obvious that the man behind the incidents was Naismith, and with his death the so-called curse ended?"

"If that is the case," I pondered, "why did he do it?"

"Jealousy, I imagine," Stoker replied. "There are so many actors who are envious of the guv'nor's talent and success that it is not terribly surprising one might try to take actions against them, particularly a lesser actor such as he."

"But the critics loved his Gonzalo in *The Tempest*, and his Polonius in *Hamlet*," Holmes said.

"Did they? Well, I wouldn't know, I ... did you say Gonzalo and Polonius?"

"I did."

"He must have played them in an amateur company, then."

"Only if you consider the Memorial Theatre in Stratford-upon-Avon to be an amateur company."

"What is it I am missing?" I interjected. "What is wrong with Naismith playing ... what were the roles again?"

"Gonzalo, in *The Tempest*, and Polonius, in *Hamlet*," Stoker said. "Both rather garrulous characters, and both rather elderly. Yet our Mr. Naismith was barely past thirty. Those two roles are traditionally played by much older actors. Then again, some actors can work miracles with face paint. Now then, Mr. Holmes, what are your fees?"

"I have performed no service, therefore I expect no remittance. Good day, Mr. Stoker."

"Oh. Well, if you change your mind, please submit an invoice. Goodbye, Mr. Holmes. Dr. Watson."

After the man had gone, I said, "That was a bit abrupt, wasn't it, Holmes?"

"There was little reason not to be abrupt, since we were wasting each other's time. Stoker's world has once more returned to its natural order, and therefore all remaining questions simply disappear, like so much smoke. A murder is dismissed as an accident and a man far too young and, apparently, far too untalented to play exacting roles is explained away by imagining him a master of theatrical cosmetics."

"You have done yourself over as old men before."

"But not on the stage, Watson! The caste system of the professional English theatre would be the envy of Indian society. The leading player may delude himself into believing he can still play Romeo at the age of seventy, particularly if he is also the company's manager, but the supporting players, those who would play Gonzalo or Polonius, accept their lot, which is to only play roles that physically suit them. You would no more find a man in his thirties playing Gonzalo as you would a bear playing Ophelia."

"So what does this mean?"

"It means that the murdered man was *not* Gabriel Naismith."

"Good lord. I can begin to see why Stoker would cling to his version of events. It is so much simpler to believe that Naismith was Naismith, that he was behind the curse, and that he accidentally fell to his death, thus causing the accidents to come to an end."

"Simpler, no question," Holmes said, "but only plausible if you do not acknowledge that Naismith, or whomever was impersonating him, was murdered."

"So what is left? This man—whoever he is—dies and the accidents end. I know your views on the supernatural, Holmes. You cannot be arguing that his death was the fulfilment of the curse."

Holmes suddenly turned on me, his eyes afire. "Watson! You inspire me! You've hit it!"

"What have I hit now?"

"The answer, if I am not mistaken. We must return to the Lyceum at our earliest convenience." Holmes wasted no time in rushing to the street and engaging a hansom cab to take us there. On the way, I said: "Now would you mind telling me what it is that you have deduced based up on my speculation?"

"You implied that Naismith's death was the ultimate fulfilment of the curse," he replied.

"Actually, I was attempting to argue that such a conclusion was absurd."

"On the contrary, Watson, it is the answer to everything. Stoker first appeared to ask that I ward off any talk of a curse. Clearly someone in the theatre had already started spreading such rumours. Then he returned, harbouring the belief that someone was attempting to destroy Irving's production of *Macbeth* from within. But what if neither Irving nor the play were the intended victim at all?"

"Who, then? Ellen Terry?"

"No, Naismith! At least the man who called himself Naismith. These so-called accidents were staged as carefully as a Shakespearean battle. The business of the falling battens, the open trap door, even the brown adder was created to convince everyone else that the curse actually existed, so that when the final act of this deadly drama occurred—the killing of Naismith—it would not seem like a slaying, but rather one more instance of the curse. Whether one believed in the curse of *Macbeth* or not, the murder was meant to be perceived as just one in a series of terrible misfortunes, rather than a deliberate, cold-blooded act. In its own diabolical way, it is rather ingenious."

Holmes said nothing more until we had arrived at the Lyceum Theatre. Upon arriving there, we proceeded straight to the cramped office of Bram Stoker. "Come in and sit down, if you can," he said. "Have you decided to present me with an invoice in person, Mr. Holmes?"

"I am afraid it did not enter my mind," Holmes replied. "I am here instead to inform you that a man has been murdered, most foully, inside this theatre."

"What? Who?"

"I do not know."

"Mr. Holmes, I'm afraid I do not understand."

"As much as can be explained will be, though it is necessary that Mr. Irving be included in this conversation."

"I'll see if he can spare the time," Stoker sighed, getting up and leaving the office. Some five minutes later, he returned with Henry Irving in tow. Irving did not appear pleased to see us.

"Still muddling in our business, are we?" he growled. "Murder indeed! There had better be a point to this."

"I will not waste your time or my words," Holmes said. "I have a proposition for you." Along with Irving and Stoker, I listened to Holmes's scheme, and I worked to stifle a laugh, because I did not for one moment believe that it would work. However, Holmes and his methods have surprised me in the past. It took all of Holmes's persuasive skills to convince the actor manager to go along with his plan, but once he had, we were able to return to Baker Street, where Holmes prepared to lay his trap.

Two days later we were back at the theatre with the entire company. This was deliberate as well, though those in the company did not realize that. Ellen Terry had stepped out onto the stage, clad in the most astonishing costume; a dress that was green and shimmering, which, I learned was the result of stitching actual beetles' wings onto the fabric. "I had best get used to moving in this," she told Irving.

For his part, Irving was hovering around a huge banqueting table on the stage, having his assistants shift it slightly to the left, then right, until he was happy with its placement. He then called for the actors he wished to be seated at the table. From the army of supernumeraries, he selected a handful—myself included, as well as the actor who had nearly removed my chin with an iron glove on my first day at the Lyceum—to fill out the scene as "lords," and then looked around and cried out, "Where is Wentham? Where is our Banquo?" An actor whose handsome countenance was that of yesterday's fiery Romeo, but whose looks had settled into a distinguished middle age, entered the stage wearing a hooded robe. "Hmmm, we shall have to see about that costume," Irving said. "A bit too ominous, I think. But that is tomorrow's problem. Take your place, if you would please."

"Yes, sir," Mr. Wentham uttered, disappearing backstage again.

Irving then turned to the rest of his cast. "All my nobles, lords, and my lady, remember that it is vital that you ignore the presence of Banquo, as you cannot see him. Now then, are my murderers in place?"

"Here, guv," called the actor who was playing the First Murderer.

"Everyone at beginners, please." Leading the cast off stage, Irving instantly transformed himself into the very picture of authority and walked back on, reciting: "You know own degrees; sit down: at first and last the hearty welcome." The actors took their places at the table, as Irving went on with the scene, conferring in an aside with his murderers, who assured him that his rival Banquo was dead, even though Banquo's son escaped. This news was greeted by Irving's Macbeth in what appeared to me to replicate a heart attack, though I imagine it was simply acting. The scene continued and at last the robed figure of Banquo, his head obscured by the hood, stepped eerily on stage and took the only empty seat at the table. Irving returned to the scene and, as Macbeth, noticed the seemingly out of place character. Then Banquo raised his head to show his face. Despite Irving's direction that everyone ignore the figure, there was a collective gasp from the cast.

"Which of you has done this?" Irving demanded, in character.

A silence had fallen over all but one of the actors: a supernumerary portraying a lord, who cried out upon seeing the face of Banquo, "No!" he cried. "This cannot be!"

"You have no lines, young man," Irving declared.

"You're dead!"

"I beg your pardon? Who is dead?"

"B-Banquo!"

"Was my direction not explicit? You are not to see him."

"But he's there!"

"That is Niall Wentham, and we are privileged to have him!"

"It's not! It's Pemberton, but ... he's dead!" the young man stammered. "I killed him! But he's come back! Right there he is! Keep him away from me!"

"Banquo" suddenly flung off his cloak and cried, "Watson!"

I rushed forward to the stricken supernumerary, training my service revolver upon him. "I would not make a move if I were you," I said, he did indeed make a move ... sinking to the floor, incapacitated from terror.

On stage, Sherlock Holmes, who had donned the robe in order to appear as Banquo, produced a cloth and vigorously wiped his face, removing the extensive but skilfully-applied disguise that had recreated the face of the man everyone in the theatre knew as Gabriel Naismith.

"My friends," Irving announced to the cast, "I am about to do something that is counter to my nature; I wish to apologize. I beg your forgiveness for whatever fright I may have put you through with this little charade. Mr. Wentham, are you backstage still?"

"I am, sir," the actor's voice called, and a moment later he stepped out onto the stage.

Irving rushed to him to shake his hand. "I thank you for your splendid duplicity."

For his part, the killer looked from face to face before settling on the freshly-revealed visage of Holmes. "Oh, God ..." he moaned, putting his head in his hands. Stoker appeared then and was instructed by Irving to once again fetch the police.

"I've already done so," Stoker replied. Then glancing at the murderer, he added: "This fellow's name is Horace Jepson. What have you been up to, you blackguard?"

"I don't have to talk," Horace Jepson said, miserably.

"Let me speak for you, then," Holmes said. "Watson, do you recognize this fellow?"

I looked at him, wondering why I should recognize him any more than the others in the theatre, and then it came to me. "Yes," I replied. "Unless I am greatly mistaken, this is the fellow who nearly sheared off my chin upon my first day here. He was wielding a sword, but inexpertly so, due to his wearing an iron gauntlet."

"Just the sort of protection one would want to wear on one's hand when handling a dangerous snake," Holmes said.

"Great Scott!" I uttered.

"Do you deny it, sir?" Holmes asked the man.

"I'm saying nothing," Jepson maintained.

"Not even why you killed Naismith?"

"His name was Pemberton, and he murdered Gabriel Naismith, my godfather, and the best man I've ever known!"

I looked to Sherlock Holmes, unable to keep the shock upon hearing this was related to the Pemberton case off of my face; he, meanwhile, remained stoic. If Jepson's revelation took him by surprise, he did not reveal it.

"You probably don't even remember, Mr. Holmes," Jepson went on, "but someone came to see you, begging you to track Pemberton. That was Gabriel's nephew, Richard, and my friend, and you threw him out!"

"Pemberton was dead by then," Holmes said.

"Bollocks, he was dead! He staged his death and then reappeared under the guise of the man he had killed. Gabriel was an actor and a fine one. His miserable killer assumed that by posing as him, he would be able to hide in plain sight, like the letter in that Poe story. Richard and I knew he was not dead, but we couldn't convince anyone, including you. So I decided to take matters into my own hands. I tracked Pemberton for months, following him here. I managed to get hired as a scenery actor, but bided my time. Right before I killed him, I told him who I was and that I knew who *he* was."

"And you staged all the 'accidents' to establish the reality of a curse," I prompted.

"I'd heard about the supposed curse of *Macbeth* from Gabriel, and thought I could use it to my advantage. I didn't want anyone else to get hurt, but I had to make the accidents appear real, so Pemberton's death would be accepted as a part of it." Jepson gazed up at Holmes. "I'm not sorry, you know. I'm not even sorry you caught on to me. I'm glad he's finally, really dead."

The police, led by our old acquaintance Gregson, entered the theatre at that moment and, after a brief explanation, took Jepson away. Turning to his actors, Irving said, "Ladies and gentlemen, since no amount of thespian activity could top the scene you have just witnessed for sheer drama, there is no use continuing. You may all leave, and God help our chances of opening on schedule." Then turning to Holmes, he smiled—an expression for which he appeared to have had little practise—and loped toward us, taking each of us by the arm. "Mr. Holmes, Dr. Watson, may I offer you a drink in the comfort of the Beefsteak Room?"

"The Beefsteak Room?" I asked.

"A private club here in the theatre."

"We shall be delighted," Holmes said.

We were escorted by Irving and Stoker to the ornate private club, which was done up to resemble a Georgian dining room, complete with a hearth and oak panelling. Portraits of such earlier actors as Garrick, Kean, and Macready adorned the walls. Irving himself poured us a fine aged brandy, while thanking us for our service. After two very pleasant hours, during which all thoughts of a curse were banished, Holmes and I arose and, after exchanging pleasantries with one of London's finest actors, took our leave. We had not gotten to the door of the theatre, however, when Bram Stoker appeared behind us. "If you have a moment, sometime, Dr. Watson, I should like to talk with you," he said. "This is about your other profession."

"I shall hail the cab, Watson," Holmes said. "You may join me when your consultation is over." He then exited the building onto Wellington Street.

"You have a medical issue?" I asked.

"Oh, no sir. What I mean is your *other* other profession, yourself as a popular writer. You see, I have written myself, nothing much, mind you, but I have had a few small things published. But of late I have been formulating this idea about a creature of the night who returns from the dead. The undead, you might say. Having witnessed the response to Mr. Holmes's appearance as Naismith leads me to believe that there might be a place for such a story on the stage, or perhaps even as a novel. I would like to see what you think of the idea."

"Oh, well, yes, feel free to call on me anytime," I said hastily. "I really must go now. Holmes hates to be kept waiting."

"He and the guv'nor are cut of the same cloth, aren't they?"

I had not really thought of things that way, but in my desire to leave, I merely smiled and then hastened out into the night. In the cab on the way back to Baker Street, I told Holmes what Stoker had confided in me.

"Will you indulge him?"

"Probably, but more out of politeness than anything else. You've been around the man. You've seen how thoroughly devoted he is to Irving. I cannot imagine Bram Stoker as his own man under any circumstance."

"Really? You believe that one must be his own man in order to write?"

"No question, Holmes. I mean, how could one be so completely under the spell of another man, so much so that he sacrifices his own identity, and still have the wherewithal to produce a literary creation? It simply cannot be."

"If you say so," Sherlock Holmes replied, with the most mysterious smile.

HERCULE POIROT'S BIRTHDAY

David Gibb

I was paging through my racing form on the couch when I could suddenly feel Poirot's piercing little eyes upon me. He sat at his desk with his palms resting on the perfectly round protrusion of his midsection and his fingers peaked in thought. He looked especially egg-shaped, and was wearing a dreadfully garish vest that made it look like he belonged in an Easter basket.

"Do you know, what is the significance of today, Hastings?" he asked with a quiet smile.

"Sure enough. My cousin Larry has a piece of a horse in the Kensington Stakes this afternoon. There was a soaking rain all through the night, and if his trainer's right, Larry's about to make a tidy sum."

"Your cousin should hope that it's his piece that crosses the finish line first, eh?" he shot back dryly.

"He's been looking for the right horse for three years—missed out on Sansovino, you know. Almost killed him."

"As long as I have been in your company, *mon ami*, I have become too familiar with the habits of your idle English gentlemen. When Hercule Poirot asks you 'What is the significance of today?' he cannot possibly be considering horses or gambling or anything that should be happening in Kensington."

"You just don't appreciate sport, Poirot. You don't understand the pride a man feels when he knows he's been part of bringing a great horse from the farm to the track."

"One must pity the horse, Hastings. For so many years, he pulls the cart and tills the field, and then just as soon as man invents machinery that can ease his burden, they jump upon his back for sport."

"Well if not the Kensington Stakes," I finally asked glumly, "what is the real significance of today?"

"*C'est mon anniversaire*," he said with proud formality.

"I say! Happy birthday, Poirot! How many is this? You must be getting on."

"My very dear Hastings," he interrupted me, "as usual, you have asked the worst possible question for the occasion. This evening, I will dine at Chez Francois in celebration. Will you join me?"

"I wouldn't miss it for the world!"

"*Bon*. And if your cousin's horse is victorious upon the mud of Kensington, I shall extend to you the honor of paying the bill."

"Of course, old chap!" I said with a laugh.

Chez Francois had only been open about two months, but it was riding high off a stellar review in the Sunday Times and had quickly become the place to be seen. Poirot, however, was unmoved by the restaurant's fashionability and instead preoccupied with the chef, the aforementioned Francois.

"This man, Francois, he has brought the true elegance of French cuisine to this damp island, my friend," he explained as he produced a golden safety pin from his vest pocket and used it to fasten his napkin just below his collar. "He brings not just the meats and sauces *tres riche* that the English know as French; he also celebrates the humble vegetables of the common people."

"Ah," was all I could manage.

"And his grandmother on his mother's side, she was Belgian, so you see, there can be no more natural man to craft *la cuisine pour Hercule Poirot*!"

Just then, there went up an awful roar at the next table over from us. There was a crashing of silverware and plates to the floor, and a few ladies gasped or let out cries of dismay.

"Someone—someone had better call a doctor!" a handsome young man shouted from the table.

There was great scampering around the room, but Hercule Poirot appeared completely indifferent to the whole scene, leaning towards the kitchen impatiently.

"The terrine here, Hastings, it has been called the finest in London."

"It looks like that woman is in some distress," I said, somewhat in disbelief at his obliviousness to the situation.

"*Pauvre femme*, it is too late for interventions. She has been poisoned with cyanide," he responded quite flatly.

"What on Earth do you mean, Poirot?" I whispered. "What's going on here? Is this a joke?"

"Unfortunately, *non*. I would not play such pranks. It is a clear inference: a girl cries out as she eats and collapses very quickly, surely she has been poisoned."

"But cyanide? You haven't even looked at her!"

"Again, a clear inference if you were to employ your gray cells and examine closely your menu," he grumbled. "Chef Francois is known for his almond *macaron*, and the adjacent table, they are enjoying dessert. The taste of the poison would not be recognized until it was too late."

"Well, we can't just sit here," I protested.

"*C'est mon anniversaire!*" he chirped in objection.

The entire restaurant sat transfixed in horror as a doctor who happened to be at Chez Francois for dinner carried out a quick examination and confirmed Poirot's conclusion: the poor girl was dead. In the stunned silence, the only sound was the sawing of Poirot's knife as he continued unfazed with his duck confit.

"If this poor girl's been murdered, don't you think we need to do something to help?" I finally asked him with some frustration.

"The time for investigation will begin when the police arrived," he explained prescriptively. "For now, it is time to salvage what enjoyment I may have left of this fine cuisine on the day of my birth."

I thought Poirot quite selfish in that moment, but he was right that any attempt to question witnesses in an organized manner before the arrival of the police would be impossible. After about twenty minutes, the tall, square figure of Chief Inspector Japp marched brusquely into the room. Poirot attempted to make himself very small in hopes that he might finish his vegetables before having to solve the murder we had just witnessed. Given the circumstances, I refused to play along and stood up to meet Japp.

"Captain Hastings!" he greeted "What seems to be the trouble here?"

"Well, the girl just cried out as she was eating and died," I explained, "and Poirot says she's been poisoned with a cyanide macaron."

"Does he, indeed?" asked the tall policeman, leaning around me to spot Poirot eating the remainder of the finest French cuisine in London as fast as he could.

Poirot finally acquiesced and, with a defeated wobble of his round head, unfastened his golden safety pin and stood up from the table.

"Surely the only logic in this case is to begin with the origin point of the food. We must speak to Chef Francois at once," he said decisively.

Moments later, we were squeezed into the narrow confines of the kitchen as Poirot questioned the chef he admired so much.

"*Monsieur le Chef*, I shall not waste your time. I am quite sure that this girl has been poisoned using your food."

"*Non, monsieur! C'est impossible!*"

"Unfortunately, I am afraid it is the only possibility. Rest assured, though, sir, I count you among the wronged in this entire affair. Your fine *cuisine* deserves better than to be besmirched by such wrongdoing. I shall clear your name as well as the name of your *macaron*!"

The chef wore the look of amazement and confusion that Japp and I had long ago learned not to give away so quickly.

"You must tell me, though, do you trust all of the waiters and waitresses here?"

"*Certainement, monsieur*. I hand selected them myself, and they all come with very good references."

"As I expected," Poirot muttered. "Let me ask: if the *macaron* is made by you, then it is not poisoned in the kitchen. If all your waiters and waitresses are trustworthy, then it is not poisoned on the way to the table. Since the table has six guests seated at it, then it is impossible to tamper with the *macaron* at the table. So when could the cyanide possibly be introduced?"

"Hold on, though," Japp intervened. "Do you hand all the plates directly to the wait staff?"

"If they are waiting there, of course we hand them," the chef replied quickly.

Poirot gazed knowingly at Japp with a twinkle in his eye.

"And if they are not there, you place them in the window between the kitchen and the dining room, is that not correct?"

"*Oui*, but they're picked up very quickly. Our wait staff is second to none."

"Indeed," Poirot said thoughtfully. "I think our murderer was very aware of that reputation. Come, Hastings. We must meet the unfortunate young lady's companions."

As we squeezed out of the narrow kitchen, I quietly posed to Poirot, "If you're sure everything's on the up-and-up with the staff, then one of these five people must be our murderer."

"*Bien sur*, Hastings. Our killer believes that by committing this act in public, he or she has hidden as a needle in the hay. However, I think we will find a clear motive for only one person," and then he added after a pause, "and that person has worn a blue silk bow tie tonight, like all the waiters."

It turned out our victim was the young Miss Patricia Primrose of Wimbledon, who had been dining with her family that evening. Japp's men had already separated them from the rest of the shocked patrons of Chez Francois.

Her parents, Peter and Emily Primrose looked like mannequins in a lady's clothing store. They were dressed in the most impressive finery, but both looked drained of any blood. Her fiancé, the young journalist Matthew Eaton, on the other hand, was red with fury and turmoil. Finally, the late Miss Primrose's cousin Elizabeth Tyler was present with her husband Reginald Tyler, the regarded winger for Wimbledon.

Poirot temporarily set up shop in Chef Francois's office, which was little more than a closet with an assortment of ledgers and handwritten notes stacked precariously on every available surface. His incredible reverence for the chef was evident, as he resisted the urge to straighten papers or square books on shelves but rather took in the room with his eyes up like a stunned tourist.

"It is true what they say about geniuses, Hastings," he remarked, laying his handkerchief down on the seat of the desk chair. "They are diverse in their ways and methods."

I admired his restraint for not saying "we."

The stunned Primroses were the first to interview with Poirot. Peter Primrose had made a small fortune importing furs from Canada and was a rugged, jowly man in spite of his somewhat delicate name. His massive frame dwarfed the devastated Emily, whose hands were pale and trembling terribly.

"Please excuse me for asking, *Madame et Monsieur*," Poirot began, "but can you think of anybody who would want to do your daughter harm?"

"Not yet, indeed!" old Peter rumbled loudly. "That Eaton's no good, but I must've been wrong about him after all."

Even Poirot seemed taken aback by Primrose's forwardness.

"You mean to say you thought it was likely *Monsieur Eaton* would hurt her sometime in the future?" he asked.

"Well, maybe in a few years, after we were both gone."

"What an awful thing to say!" the ghostly white Emily wailed.

The old man glowered at her, and she shrunk back into her sobbing.

"Patricia would've done well when myself and the missus were done with our business here," he explained gruffly. "I'm not saying Eaton didn't have his eye on her money, but I also think he'd be smart enough—and patient enough—to wait until she was worth more, if he was going to try anything like that."

"My word!" I ejaculated.

"No, Hastings. Mr. Primrose, I think he understands the value of transparency in these proceedings. If he speaks too plainly, it is only his grief and his eagerness for justice," Poirot corrected.

"Right. Sorry," I allowed.

The aforementioned Mr. Matthew Eaton was next.

"Mr. Eaton, I must extend to you my highest condolences," Poirot opened.

"Yes. Right. Thank you," the young man responded with his eyes cast downward.

"How did you and Miss Primrose first meet?"

"I was covering the dedication of the new library last year, and she was there representing her family, who had, um," and he paused, fidgeting for a second, "well, footed the bill for the place, you know."

"So you knew she was a very rich woman before you fell in love."

"Well, sure," he responded, "but I don't see what difference that would make."

"Prevent my saying this, *Monsieur*, but some might suggest that if you loved her money more than you loved her, then removing her would've been a convenience."

"Is that what her parents are saying?" Eaton shot back with renewed flush.

"*Non.* Indeed, her father has absolved you."

"Really?" he asked with surprise that seemed genuine. "That's the first nice thing old Beaver Pete's ever said about me."

"He believes you are too dishonest to have committed this crime, sir. He thinks you would've laid in wait with a more grandiose scheme," Poirot corrected.

Eaton knitted his brow combatively. "Would you like to hear about a grandiose scheme, Mr. Poirot? Imagine paying duties for a single crate of pelts and unloading an entire ship. In my investigations, I have uncovered—"

"So you were investigating Peter Primrose's business the entire time you were engaged to his daughter?" I asked with some disgust.

"They're not mutually exclusive!" he insisted.

Finally, Reginald and Elizabeth Tyler came in to speak with Poirot. They shared the space much better than the Primroses, and Reginald had his arm around his wife in a way that was both supportive and jocular.

"Look, I don't suppose we could get out of here anytime soon," Reginald broke in. "I've very eager to get to the wireless or the evening paper."

"You've a horse in the Kensington Stakes," I said knowingly.

"Yes, indeed—well, a piece of one—"

"Honestly," Elizabeth broke in, "I can't imagine a more unimportant thing to talk about today than a horse race!"

"I could not agree more, Mrs. Tyler," Poirot soothed. "I have already had this conversation with the rather insensitive Captain Hastings once today. Tell me, *Madame*, what is your opinion of your cousin's fiancé?"

"I believe he is a thoroughly rotten man," she began, "but Patricia was frightfully in love with him."

"And you, *Monsieur*?" he directed to Reginald.

"I found him to be the sort of journalist who wants to talk to you after you lost a match. Just no decency at all," he said, before adding, "Good story teller, though. I think he's very good at social events and such."

After a thoughtful pause, Poirot asked directly, "Do you think he would kill her?"

"Absolutely not. Everybody loved Patricia and wanted the best for her," Elizabeth replied with an earnest smile.

"Lovely girl," Reginald echoed with a shrug.

After the couple had left the tiny office, Poirot caught the attention of Japp's young sergeant, whispered something into his ear, and then directed all of us back into the dining room. He had the unfortunate family members return to their original seats and placed me in the chair that had been occupied by Patricia.

"Patricia Primrose, soon to be Patricia Eaton, was loved by many people," he began. "Her parents adore her and seek to protect her from evil. Her cousin loves her dearly. Even her fiancé, misguided and selfish as his motivations often are, can't deny that he is truly in love with her."

"Hold on just a second here," Eaton objected.

"Shut up and let the man talk, Matthew," Primrose interjected.

"Ah, but see, that brings us perfectly to young Miss Patricia's problem," Poirot explained. "Her father and her future husband are both awful men."

"Where the hell do you get off saying things like that?" Primrose rumbled, suddenly even more indignant than his much-maligned son-in-law.

"For many years, *Monsieur*, you have dominated your wife. I have spoken to you for just minutes, and I see the look of fear and sadness in her eyes. She is never free in your presence."

All eyes went to Mrs. Primrose, whose sad, pallid complexion and downcast gaze gave sad confirmation to Poirot's words.

"You should mind your bloody business and watch what you say," Peter responded, his eyes welling up with frustration. "Someone's killed my daughter right in front of me, and I'll be damned if I'm going to sit around and be accused of things I have not done."

"Have no fear, sir," Poirot said with flat contempt, "I am not here to accuse you of murder. However, you have certainly inspired one."

There was a collective din of disbelief.

"*Monsieur* Primrose, for years, you treat your wife with utter disrespect and cruelty, even in front of your own child. Yet somehow, through the grace of God, your daughter, she grows up vital and beautiful and seems unmarked by your terribleness.

"Then one day, *Monsieur*, she falls in love with a young man. A young man who is too much like you," Poirot continued. "A terrible man, who was already using your daughter before he was even married to her to benefit his own career. A man you said yourself was playing—how do you say—the long con."

"I would never harm her—or even him!" Primrose insisted.

"No, you wouldn't. You very clearly showed me yourself that you were content to sit back and let Matthew Eaton unravel your daughter's life however he saw fit."

"Alright, Poirot," Japp finally asserted, "it's time to stop talking about who didn't kill Patricia Primrose and get to the point."

"It is not yet clear, Chief Inspector?" Poirot asked with some whimsy. "Mrs. Elizabeth Tyler said it the best herself: 'Everybody loved Patricia and wanted the best for her.' Given the impending horror of her poorly-chosen marriage, Patricia Primrose was killed by the person who loved her most in an act of misguided mercy."

Finally, Poirot focused his attention on Emily Primrose, whose fading figure suddenly seemed stronger and more defined.

"You, *Madame*. You have acted out of love, but you have done a horrible thing."

"How could she not have known better?" the sad-eyed Emily replied. "She grew up in her father's house, and yet she dives headfirst into marriage with a man who tells her where to go and what to do and which causes to donate to."

"Emily!" Mr. Primrose objected as he recoiled away from his long-suffering wife.

"So you took advantage of the fact you and your husband had been to Chez Francois before. You wore a white blouse and obtained a blue bowtie to match the uniform you knew the staff here wore. Between the main course and dessert, you excuse yourself to the ladies room, remove your outer garments and put on the bowtie, allowing you to pass for a waitress. For so many years, your husband had made you invisible. You learned the lessons well.

"Disguised in plain sight, you approach the window between the kitchen and the dining room and find the plate of *macarons* you know are for your table. Using your motherly insight, you even identify which color *macaron* Patricia would claim and poison just the one."

"Aunt Emily!" Elizabeth cried out, her eyes welling up.

At that moment, Japp's sergeant entered the dining room with a small black and gold cylinder in his hand.

"Ah," Poirot explained, "the young sergeant has been kind enough to retrieve for me the wastebasket from the ladies' washroom. In it, you will see, we find the blue bowtie worn by our killer entangled with the tissue you used to reapply your lipstick."

The whole of the room turned to Emily Primrose.

"Well, someone had to help her. It was the only thing left to do."

"These are not your decisions to be made, *madame*!" Poirot instructed sharply. "Your daughter would have understood that Matthew Eaton was not a good man in her own time, and then you could've helped her. Instead, you denied her the chance to ever be happy again because you were so sure she would be unhappy."

Japp nodded to his sergeant, who conducted Mrs. Primrose out of the restaurant. Within a few minutes, the restaurant had emptied out, leaving only Poirot, myself, and the still-stunned owner of the establishment.

"*Monsieurs*, I must thank you very much for clearing this up so quickly before it could get into any of the papers."

"Ah, of course *mon chef*, I told you I would preserve both your reputation and that of your very fine restaurant," Poirot replied with a smile.

"Speaking of papers," I jumped in, "I'd love to see an evening edition. The results of the Kensington Stakes should have come in."

"*Non,* Hastings. Our work here is not yet done," Poirot clucked. "Chef Francois, we still must taste your famous almond *macaron*."

THE ADVENTURE OF THE VERY QUIET AMERICAN

Eric Cline

"D r. Watson! Come here. I want you."

"Pardon?"

Holmes waved a letter that had been delivered by courier.

"A policeman down in Kent needs my services. Its nature requires your skills."

This was certainly flattering! I had gained some measure of "reflected" glory due to my published chronicles of Holmes's more challenging cases. Boswell must not overshadow Johnson; yet I straightened perceptibly with pride.

"I need you to examine a badly mangled corpse," Holmes said.

My nose crinkled. I had studied as needed at the University of London to take my degree, but I would never miss the smell of the mortuary.

"Oh, come now, Watson. Buck up. This is your field of expertise."

"I am no Monsieur Dupin," I said, jokingly mentioning the fictional detective. But then I allowed: "Of course, I do know a thing or two."

"There's the spirit!" Holmes jumped up out of his chair and retrieved a valise; he began packing various tobaccos, a couple of fine pipes, and even some clothing.

An Inspector Arthur McGann was the author of the letter. His purview included the unincorporated farms and estates of the village of Penshurst and its surrounding area. Sir Bernard P.B. Earley, proprietor of the Robinette estate, had been found dead under the most horrid of circumstances. As I read the note, I realized that this was the bit of sensation that the more vulgar papers had trumpeted the other day; it was the fellow who had been eaten by his own pigs.

Very little of the body remained, but it had been conclusively identified. Sir Earley had been missing for a single night before his remains were discovered in a pig trough, in a condition one could indelicately describe as *Requiem in Frusta.*

There was another detail that made me blush.

"I see you just reached the part regarding the man staying with them," Holmes said from across the room.

"How did you ...?"

"Your eyebrows shot up at that exact instant, old man. You just realized there might be some of what you have previously referred to as 'vulgar intrigue.'" He chuckled as he cracked the chamber on his revolver and inspected it. Then it too went into a valise.

Vulgar intrigue, indeed. The main house was now occupied by only two persons, according to McGann; the widow, Viola Earley, and an American visitor named Bryce Perkins. McGann's words made little pretense of hiding what he suspected. Viola was "not yet thirty years of age," while her late husband had been "just shy of fifty." Bryce Perkins was "a fit and handsome young rake, perhaps thirty-five at most." Further, McGann wrote, "I fear they have arranged a 'story' to account for the death." He did not elaborate on why they would have thus colluded, but his suspicions could hardly have been more obvious.

"Remember, Watson, keep an open mind," Holmes said. "Inspector McGann has given us all of his notions packed neatly in a box, but you must not let that colour your own thinking. Viola Earley may or may not be a Madame Bovary, but we cannot know until we do our own investigations. Say now, are you going to start packing, or not?"

We took the train to Royal Tonbridge Wells; from there, McGann would meet us with a coach for the drive to Penshurst. Fortunately, passengers were few, and we had a compartment to ourselves. We were able to discuss the case with utmost privacy.

"We know that the American Bryce Perkins has not acted in any overtly untoward fashion," Holmes said. "Clearly, he knows how to avoid being gossiped about. We can be assured that Viola Earley and Perkins have *not* been seen walking about in Kent, hand in hand."

McGann's letter had contained no such assurances. I sighed, knowing I would have to ask the inevitable question: "What makes you think that, Holmes?"

As usual, my friend looked surprised that a mere mortal could not follow the clues which seemed so clearly marked.

"Why, the papers of course. They made a brief sensation of the fact that an apparent accidental death had resulted in a wealthy landowner being eaten by his own pigs. You saw that as well as I. But if there had been even the slightest hint among the local inhabitants that Bryce Perkins was some sort of illicit paramour to Lady Earley, well, some enterprising Fleet Street hack journalist would have gotten wind of it. It would be continuing sensation amongst evening editions and special editions.

"And this train car from London, rather than being quiet enough for us to talk in peace, would be packed by scribblers from all of the papers, bound for Penshurst village.

"Q.E.D., Bryce Perkins's public conduct during the time he has been a guest in the Earley home has been that of a choirboy. He has surely been mild-mannered and self-effacing."

"Oh, yes." Say this for my mercurial friend: no matter how mysterious his ways, whenever he laid out his evidence, we ordinary *homo sapiens* could all see it, after the fact.

"Right then, Holmes. What does your deductive faculty tell you about late Sir Earley?"

"Good Lord, Watson. I enjoy cogitation, but not shoveling sand uphill. I didn't deduce. Directly upon receiving the letter, I consulted my Debrett's Peerage."

"Ah," I smiled. Sir Earley, as a knight of the realm, would be listed there, along with some dry bits of biography; the book was on the shelf of every upper class English home. "Well, I would say that's quite a bit more than I know, Holmes. So, is it Bernard Earley or Barry Earley? I have seen both names used by yesterday's papers."

Holmes clapped his hands together forcefully. "I am genuinely impressed!" And I think he was. "You have hit upon the heart of the matter!"

"Mm. Well, I may have hit on it, Holmes, but rather as a blind man driving a stake into the ground, I find that I'm not sure if I can hit it a second time, or even what *it* is."

"The man called 'Sir Barry Earley' was christened Bernard Praisegod Barebone Earley. He appears to have allowed himself to be addressed as 'Barry.'"

"Praisegod Barebone!"

"... Earley." Holmes added.

"Why Holmes, I know that name!"

"Of course you do, Watson. Your primary school education was admirably sound."

"Praisegod Barebone was the name of a figure within Cromwell's puritan revolution over two hundred years ago! Due to the unchecked religious fanaticism of the time, the family called Barebone gave their son that quite ludicrous first name."

"Yes, and when Charles the First was beheaded, and Cromwell had won the day, Praisegod Barebone presided over the legislative session forever after known as the Barebone Parliament. And, according to Debrett's, the Earleys were related to that figure. Bernard Praisegod Barebone Earley was the last descendant of a family that proudly kept that Cromwellian name going for two hundred years after the Stuart Restoration."

My mind raced. "But, *Sir* Bernard Praisegod Barebone Earley? How was the family possibly knighted, considering its association with the regicidal government of Cromwell? Even today, our schoolbooks and histories have not made peace with Cromwell's legacy. How could that family possibly have a knighthood to pass down to this man?"

"They didn't, Watson. The man whose body we are going to see, Bernard Praisegod Barebone Earley, was the one who was knighted. He did not inherit his title."

That made a little more sense. One of the confusing bits about knighthoods is their inheritability. If you meet "Sir Jonathan Yeoman" on the street, you don't know if he was knighted himself, or if he inherited it from a grandfather knighted eighty years ago, or from an ancestor knighted eight hundred years ago. The proliferation of "knights" of modest means, some of them descended from men who had merely built breweries or bridges, has been such a gusher that it has quite debased the currency, so to speak. Holmes once joked that if it keeps up, they will be granting knighthoods to stage actors!

"He served in the Crimean War," Holmes said. "Quite valiantly, I understand. Cited for carrying a wounded colonel on his shoulder to safety from behind the Russian lines. Very much earned his knighthood."

"Indeed."

The mention of war, reminded me of my own service in Afghanistan. My old wound began to itch—purely a trick of the mind—I distanced it from my thoughts, and consciously ordered myself to forget even its location.

"So you see, we have a rather good picture of the mind of Sir Barry Earley, as he liked to style himself."

I now began to get a glimmer of what Holmes meant, but merely nodded for him to continue.

"A son of a long anti-Royalist dynasty—a family which has proudly kept its association with the Cromwell revolution for some two hundred years, through passing along the family name—decides for himself that he wishes to be a Royalist. War service earns him a knighthood. He obscures the name as best he can by encouraging the address of 'Bernard Earley' or, alternately, Barry Earley. There is some family money; we'll have to inquire as to its source. He owned an estate in Penshurst, so he's no pauper. This tells us that he strives for respectability. Strangely, he has an American acquaintance as a guest in his home."

"Why 'strangely'?"

"Imagine, Watson, if you had managed to climb your way onto the rolls of the Knights of the Realm, after a two-hundred-year family history of defiant Puritanism. Why would you then associate yourself with a citizen of a country so steeped in republicanism that its constitution forbids the granting of titles of nobility?"

"The upper classes think nothing of it," I protested. "Members of the House of Lords have taken American wives. Lord Randolph Churchill has a Yankee wife."

He waved away my objection.

"You are talking about persons who are secure on their perch. Sir Barry Earley had nothing backing him. Nothing. So, if this was the path he chose, he had to be a fanatic about it. Mark my words, Watson. The American visitor is the key to this whole business."

Inspector McGann met us at the station with a carriage. We talked further as we were whisked to the estate.

"The most famous estate in this area is, of course, Penshurst itself," McGann told us. His accent betrayed no Scots ancestry, but his fiery whiskers mixed with frost told the tale. "It is a magnificent work of fourteenth century architecture, and subject of the well-known poem by Ben Jonson. But the Robinette estate is rather impressive in its own right. Jonson could have written his poem about that as easily. Smaller, but still a stone castle. Quite lovely. Shame to be showing it to you under such circumstances."

"It was uninhabited before Sir Earley purchased it?" Holmes said.

"Matter of fact it was. Last member of the family, all of that. I was a boy, in fact. A cousin took possession, but never inhabited it. Had better lodgings in the South of France, I hear. Probably relieved when he sold it."

Robinette Manor was smaller than Penshurst, which I have seen in sketches. But it was made of the same broad stones. I fancied you could match chisel marks on its surface with a corresponding depression in some mined-out quarry nearby. Three stories it was, a grey eminence with trellised vines and grass just barely in need of cutting.

"Old Robinette claimed, when I was a boy, that his ancestors had served William the Conqueror," McGann said. "Whether it was true or not, the family's done now." I nodded, suddenly struck by an image of entire encyclopaedias of family history, burned before my own birth.

"The papers made no mention of the source of Earley's wealth," said Holmes. "Do you know, McGann?"

"No. I assumed it was family money. Where else?"

Where else, indeed. For a substance so vital to our well being, money is something we English seem faintly embarrassed about. If one does not have the good taste to be born with it, the acquisition of it seems somehow an abrogation of manners.

"Oh well, the American will know," Holmes said. "I am not so sure about the wife."

I started to ask Holmes how he had deduced that, but then I realized that it had to be true.

The last person who knew the true financial health of a gentleman's estate was his wife.

And if anyone would be vulgar and socially inept enough to inquire about money, it would have to be an American.

Viola Earley was quite the lovely woman, but haggard as is proper for a recent widow to be. Her hair and dress were unruffled, but her skin had a grey tone that suggested many sleepless nights. The American guest was already sitting in an ill-lit corner of the parlor when we arrived.

Bryce Perkins dressed like a slightly better off tradesman of these isles might; I confess, I had half-expected him to be draped in romance novel "rake" clothing, of the sort that the chaps who strutted about Rotten Row sported; but I remembered how Holmes had proven that the man surely could not have presented the outward aspect of a seducer.

Inspector McGann showed a commendable directness. "This is all very awkward, but it must be done. Lady Earley, you know that I have questioned the manner of your husband's death. And that I have engaged the services of Mr. Sherlock Holmes," he gestured to me as well, "and the medical talents of Dr. John Watson. I wish to have enough evidence before I gather an inquest jury, so that they can decide for themselves whether to bring back a verdict of 'accidental death.'"

Mrs. Earley nodded. "It is what you must do," she said.

"What is this 'inquest jury,' exactly?" said Perkins. "I don't believe we have it in America."

It was Lady Earley who answered him. "It will be a local panel of townspeople, Mr. Perkins. Men of sober reputation from the community. These are the men who I have purchased my groceries from, the cobbler I have been fitted with shoes by, perhaps the veterinarian I have sent for to look at a sick horse in the past. All of these men whom I have hired, and who have nodded to me and tipped their hats to me in the street."

She was crestfallen, as well she might be; an inquest had the ability to upset the social order; at the very least, it gave life-and-death power to the locksmith or the greengrocer. "They shall gather together to hear the evidence presented by the constable, and shall decide whether to bring back a verdict of accidental death—or not. If they decide it was death by foul play, then the authorities will investigate further and charge one or both of us with his murder. Isn't that right, Mr. Holmes?"

"Quite so, Lady Earley," said Holmes.

Bryce Perkins had a steady gaze. He looked towards us as he spoke.

"All right, then. We don't have that in the States, at least not in Kenetakit," (His hometown, I suppose). "It's only the jury at trial where you bring in the bumbling amateur citizens."

"You think poorly of a 'jury of your peers'?" Holmes said.

"I think poorly of a great number of things about my country, Mr. Holmes. It is one of the reasons I am here. I originally struck up my friendship with Barry when I addressed a meeting he attended. We are both socialists, you see."

McGann and I exchanged looks, but Holmes merely nodded.

"I had wondered if he had gotten round to that yet," said Holmes.

"Gotten round?" Lady Earley said.

"Your late husband showed all of the signs of a man attempting to try on various identities," said Holmes. "Born into an anti-monarchist household, he gained military glory, then attempted to become a member of the upper classes, and succeeded after a fashion. He made money on his own, which I would like to hear about further, but then, perhaps in response to the subtle japes he received from the old money—the true aristocracy—began his inevitable flirtation with socialism. Do you know how he made his money, Lady Earley?"

"Of course, I do, Mr. Holmes. It was the buying and selling of bonds."

"From what foundational capital?"

"Pardon?" she said.

"Bonds are a low interest item, for the most part," Holmes said. "They are a good way to safeguard a large amount of capital, but not so much to multiply it."

"I don't know. He had mostly retired from it by the time we married. All I know is, he made his fortune in national bonds, England's and other countries'."

Holmes turned to Perkins. The American seemed to be almost a wax figure like those in Mrs. Tussaud's museum (which had moved from Baker Street just a few years before Holmes and I took up lodgings), staring straight ahead, barely blinking.

"Do you know the source of the Earley fortune, Mr. Perkins?"

Perkins cleared his throat and said: "Yes. My friend and I talked about it many a time. He wasn't too proud of it, in retrospect. It was French national debt, Mr. Holmes. Taken out in 1871."

Holmes, McGann and I uttered exclamations. Lady Earley sighed.

"You know the significance of the date, of course," Perkins continued. "It was the year France lost its war with Prussia. Barry was a middling bond trader at that time, having been introduced to it by an Army acquaintance after the Crimean war. All these damn wars!" I nodded sadly. "But he saw his opportunity for a killing then. After the siege of Paris started—that is, after everyone knew that the French were going to lose—he convinced a group of like-minded conspirators to buy French government bonds. Of course, at that point, they were going at pennies on the dollar—er, or whatever, farthings on the pound, you use here—and they were able to leverage their own resources to buy bonds that, on their face, were worth close to a million French francs."

"Good God!" someone cried. With embarrassment, I realized it was me. "They would have been no better than scrap-paper. And that would have been before the peace settlement, where the French were forced to pay reparations to the Germans! Surely they defaulted."

"Actually, they didn't," Holmes muttered.

"That's right, the French ultimately honoured their bonds," Perkins said. "But what mattered was that, *at the time*, so many traders feared they would renege on payments. But Barry knew something of the Gallic temperament, from having fought alongside Frenchmen during the Crimean War. France, after suffering defeat at the hands of the Prussians, did not want the further disgrace of being a pariah of the world's stock exchanges. They made good. But by then, Barry and his co-conspirators had bought up bonds at about ten percent of face value."

"Quite the mercenary," Inspector McGann remarked. "One wonders if any of those men who lost out when he took over their notes held a grudge." Holmes, I noticed, merely smiled at that remark.

"It's the capitalist system of buy and sell!" Perkins said. He almost became animated, as men are wont to do when they have a pre-set formula of words that they can apply to a situation, no matter the relevancy; I have noticed that socialists and the barmier Christian divines have that in common.

But then he sat back in his chair, with a visible effort. I did not know what to make of his strange posture.

"After splitting the profits with his chums, he must have cleared a profit beyond a hundred-thousand pounds," Holmes said. I gasped at that figure, but Perkins nodded.

"Good Lord, it's a wonder he didn't buy Penshurst itself!" McGann said.

"He had a better idea of what to do with the remainder of the money," Perkins said. "I am proud to say that my friend has underwritten Socialist newspapers, rented meeting halls, made bail when our comrades have been unjustly gaoled. He is—was—a very important behind-the-scenes player in this country's movement of liberation. I came here to work with him, and help export the revolution to America."

"And you were here the day he was found?" Holmes said.

"Yes, but only just. I had been away on business for the movement, in London, for several weeks. I came back the day before he died to find him very unwell."

We talked with the servants before we left. They lived in a few cottages nearby; none stayed in the main house at night. They confirmed that Sir Barry had been ill for some time, and had only spoken to them through the oaken door of his bedchamber, mainly to request meals.

It didn't take a Sherlock Holmes to see that this all sounded suspicious—but what did it add up to? My mind ran with wild notions: that perhaps it was Bryce Perkins whose half-chewed body we had examined, and that Sir Barry Earley had assumed his identity! But didn't the whole town, including McGann, know his face?

I was sure that Holmes had gotten further than I; but as was his custom, he said not a word.

We examined the body the next day.

Inspector McGann had done an excellent bit of work in preserving the evidence.

Two bodies were on ice in a special room in the mortuary near the constable station in the town itself.

One of them was Sir Bernard Earley.

The other was one who, in a sense, had been killed by him.

"When we got there that day, the hired men had pulled Earley's body away from the pig trough," McGann said. "Supposedly, it was Mr. Perkins that discovered the body. He saw four pigs feasting away and killed them with a revolver belonging to Earley. Then he went back inside and sat in the parlor, 'emotionally drained' as he put it. And, as you'll see, they'd done quite a bit of feasting before they were shot. At first, it seemed purely an accident, but then, well ..."

"Then the *second* victim died," said Holmes. "Very admirable of you to have drawn the correct conclusions, sir."

There was room to walk and work between the two slabs. Regrettably, no gas works had made it out this far, so we were illuminated only by a few lanterns.

Some large metal basins held ice, covered in sawdust. As the ice melted, the basin was drained, scraped of the sawdust, and refilled. By this method the room was chilled and the two bodies were preserved against further decay.

Sir Barry Earley's earthly remains, dressed in some muddy rags, were half a face, a torso, gnawed arms, and a bit of lower torso and thighbone; it was a grisly business. I made a brief examination of that fact, but I could not help drawing my eyes towards the second victim.

She was completely intact.

She was also *Sus scrofa domesticus*.

A domestic pig.

"Bryce Perkins supposedly shot and killed four pigs because they wouldn't leave the body alone," McGann told us, his breath making little clouds. "And there they were, all dead. But there was another one, a little ways away, with blood on its maw, who began to grow ill as I and my men stood there. Aye, Mr. Holmes, I don't have your keen senses, but I smelled the rat. The pig grew tipsy and collapsed. I went inside and discussed it with Perkins, who was still sitting down and looking strangely calm. He said that Sir Earley had somehow fallen in there and been eaten, but I had some half-formed suspicions that I need you to prove. When I told him I'd witnessed another pig collapse and die, he looked like he'd bit down on a rotted lemon."

"You suspected Earley had been poisoned," Holmes said. He ran an almost possessive hand over the body of the swine. "If Earley had died of poisoning, then Perkins knew that the pigs which had partaken of the flesh would soon fall down and die, so he shot them to cover that up. But this one had wandered out of sight. He missed her."

"Aye."

"Excellent work sir," I added.

"Work's not excellent until it's done," McGann said. He had a Scotsman's pedigree, that was for sure. "If this is poison, how do we prove it? We've no chemical laboratory here. But to hear tell, you've written encyclopaedias on the subject, Mr. Holmes."

"Merely a couple of well-received monographs, but thank you. I do not know until we do the laboratory work, but we do have our kit with us."

"I suspect that the pig's stomach shall be more likely to retain traces of the poison," I said. "If we find any."

Holmes added, without elaboration: "And, of course, there are the muddy rags Earley wore."

The next three days were pure toil. My surgeon's hands took samples of Sir Earley's remains, and extracted the stomach of the pig; Holmes performed chemical re-agent tests in a well-ventilated room set up for him by the constabulary. We stayed at McGann's home (and I pay tribute here to Mrs. McGann's cooking); there was no question of sleeping at Robinette Manor. No invitation had been given.

When I asked Holmes whether it would be helpful to be under their roof, to be nearer to the mystery, he chuckled: "No need to rummage around looking for secret safes behind portraits, Watson. Nor hidden rooms behind bookcases." I blushed as my friend teased my romantic nature.

On the third morning, a number of periodicals and letters arrived by courier from London, in response to requests by Holmes. One letter was from his brother, Mycroft, which he showed me; Mycroft's extensive contacts in every government ministry confirmed that Sir B. P. B. Earley had been decorated in the Crimea, had made a fortune in French bonds, and had been the talk of much worried speculation among high circles for his quiet financial support of radical causes. So, he was all that he had been represented to be.

Mycroft had closed his letter with: "Of course, you are to show this to no-one, but I will tell you on the QT that more than one highly-placed minister has told me they are relieved to hear of his demise. Please burn this letter immediately upon digesting its contents."

As I finished reading it and looked up, Holmes said, "Well, go ahead and burn it, Watson. You wouldn't want me sharing it with anyone." I reddened, not so much with embarrassment, but with deep feeling at the totality of my friend's trust.

The periodicals he had sent for were mostly back issues of the socialist rags. These were of interest for, although they mentioned Sir Earley not at all, they not only mentioned but illustrated the speeches of Mr. Bryce Perkins. I shall give a sample of one in particular, so striking was it in the context of our visit to Robinette Manor:

Our brother from across the Atlantic, Bryce Perkins, gave a rafter-shaking speech to the workers last night. Comrade Perkins, a distinguished American journalist, began his speech by throwing his hands out wide and yelling: "The sick and the lame must be cared for!" He then jumped out from behind the podium, and flexed his arms in a posture of strength. "I say this not out of self-interest. For I have never been ill a day in my life! I am willing to pay for free hospitals for the working poor. But the selfish capitalists, who weary their private physicians with their imaginary ills or their well-earned gout, refuse to do the same!"

Accompanying it was an illustration, which did quite a good job of capturing Perkins's likeness, showing him prancing about on stage. My lurid notion of Bernard Earley impersonating Perkins ended there. It was clearly his face. Yet ...

"I can hardly reconcile the animated man described here and the solemn waxwork man we met."

"Yes, curious that," Holmes said. He stuffed his pipe idly, sighed, and walked out the door; for Mrs. McGann did not allow smoking in the home. It was her one imperfection.

On the late afternoon of the third day, Holmes had quite the revelation. Summoning McGann to the makeshift chemical laboratory, he said, "There is no question as to the poison. It is there, in both the surviving tissues of Sir Barry Earley, and in the stomach of the pig."

"What is it?" Inspector McGann and I uttered variations on that phrase at the same instant.

"It is formaldehyde."

We were both startled into silence.

"It is certainly a poison," Holmes said. "And readily available. But hardly efficient."

"I should say not," I replied. "The victim would expire, but slowly, and in anguish, and could raise quite a row in the process. I don't believe I have ever heard of it being used for such a reason!"

"There is something you both should know," McGann said. "Lady Earley's father is a mortician. I don't know him, because his funeral parlor is in a town closer to London, but Sir Barry had bragged a bit that he chose a wife outside of the aristocracy, and mentioned her family for that reason. She was an assistant in the parlor, in fact, before she married him."

"Well, there's easy access," Holmes said. "She could have asked her father for it, or stolen it. But it scarcely matters."

"What?" said McGann.

"The salient question is not where they got the formaldehyde. It is why they used it."

"To poison him, of course," I said.

Holmes looked surprised, as he always does at the driveling of us mere mortals. "Poisoned? My dear Watson, by the time they injected him with the formaldehyde, he was already dead!"

Holmes would not explain himself further, no matter how much Inspector McGann persisted. Instead, he asked that we return to Robinette Manor for one last questioning of Viola Earley and Bryce Perkins. Rather ominously, he asked that a couple of stout policemen be taken along in case there was any difficulty.

He then took me aside in private and asked me to perform a task during the final interview. It was a most bizarre request, but knowing Holmes, I readily agreed.

"Just after you scratch your ear?" I asked.

"*Immediately* after I scratch my ear," Holmes said solemnly.

Viola Earley was, if anything, chillier of expression. Bryce Perkins again sat stoically in the shadows, betraying no more movement than one of the paintings on the walls.

"Since I engaged Mr. Holmes to consult for the law, I shall allow him 'the floor,'" Inspector McGann said.

Holmes puffed a new peach tobacco that he had just begun experimenting with. "The issue at hand is the time and manner of death of Sir Bernard Praisegod Barebone Earley." It was the first time I had heard him utter that full name since we had arrived in Penshurst. "A man whose journey through the world was quite extraordinary, and in many ways admirable. A middle-class lad from a fanatically anti-monarchist family, he earned a knighthood through battlefield bravery. His brain, and perhaps a certain want of scruple, got him his fortune, and his estate. It is not a common path in England, even if it is very much the cliché in America, Mr. Perkins."

Perkins merely shrugged silently.

"But, having found his way into the aristocracy through a rare path, a certain self-reflection, perhaps guilt, set in. He became a socialist on the QT. His activities are known in Whitehall, of course." Lady Earley startled visibly upon mention of our nation's government.

"My husband was quiet about such things," Lady Earley said. "But he did commit funds, that is certain."

I quietly walked to the other side of the room, so that I was at a triangle with Holmes and the policemen at one point, and Viola Earley and Bryce Perkins at another. And I waited.

"Yes he did, Lady Earley," Holmes said. "Funds to help comrades such as Mr. Perkins here travel the world, funds to publish newspapers, funds for bailment of gaoled protestors, a great deal of money. Even his own deep pockets must have been strained by it."

"How dare you!" she said, although I noticed that there was no real shock in her voice. It was very much the *pro forma* attempt at outrage. "It is true that Barry was spending down our capital, and if he had kept going at this rate, all would be gone within ten years. But I talked with him about it, wife to husband, and he agreed that he was going to scale it back to reasonable levels."

Holmes gave a languid shrug. "As you say, Madam."

He scratched his ear.

"Ak!" I yelled from across the room. My brief screech brought turned heads and astonished looks from all parties (save Holmes). "Sorry," I said quickly. "Some dreadful twinge in my throat. Must have it looked at soon."

"By a real doctor," Bryce Perkins muttered. I reddened.

"The story of Sir Earley's death is this: that in a state of dissolution, he died when he wandered over to the pig barn and collapsed among them. And yes, pigs are dangerous animals. Good thing you shot the infernal beasts, Mr. Perkins."

"Barry had been both ill and drunk for several days," the wife said.

"Yes, so ill that he had not been *seen* for several days," Holmes said. "Merely heard, through doors. Very kind of you to deliver his meals to him and empty his chamber pot, Lady Earley."

"He was my husband."

"Was he?" Holmes said. "Was the voice heard through thick oaken doors for several days truly your husband?"

"What are you implying?" she said. "Who else could it be?"

Holmes withdrew a news clipping supplied by Mycroft from a vest pocket. "From 'British Worker,' one of the sheets your husband so kindly funded, from April the last." He began to read.

"'Gifted orator Bryce Perkins addressed the Quarrymens' Association the previous Saturday. It was an excellent speech, interrupted numerous times. He called for greater co-operation amongst workers on both sides of the Atlantic. Although Brother Perkins is an American, he did note-perfect mockery of several of the Tory villains at Downing Street and Whitehall. So good were his impersonations, you would have almost thought the capitalist reactionaries had themselves dared to appear on stage at a gathering of honest workers.'"

Holmes put away the paper, having made his point. "You have the talent to impersonate Sir Earley, Mr. Perkins. Furthermore, the fact that the body was pumped full of formaldehyde," and here he looked toward Lady Earley, "something that would have been of little trouble to an undertaker's daughter," and here the lady knitted her hands together, not meeting Holmes's gaze, "argues for the fact that he was killed days, possibly weeks, before his body was thrown to the pigs, and hidden on the property. There was a stain on the remaining clothing that, at first, I thought was merely mud.

"But part of it was, in fact, sawdust, as is used to pack blocks of ice for keeping food—or corpses—from spoiling. I scraped mud off the rags and found sawdust *under* it; meaning it was already on the clothing before he was dumped into the mud. He had already been on ice, in some hidden room in the manse, before he was dragged out in the open, on this estate, just before the dawn, to be devoured by the pigs. And the pigs then shot dead by the dear friend who was so angered at their swinish desecration. Pity about that one who ate her fill early and wandered away unnoticed.

"But if this was a plot between you to murder him, why the complications? Why kill him weeks ago, and go to the ghastly trouble and risk of hiding the corpse, preserving it with ice and formaldehyde, and impersonating his voice, and all of that, just to dump his body on the grounds?

"No, I do not believe the murder itself was planned. One point in both your favours."

Viola Earley scowled and looked at the floor. Bryce Perkins had his eyes closed, and a tear fell from his left eyelid.

"I believe it was all a horrible, unexpected row. Perhaps Sir Earley caught the two of you in ... an indelicate embrace. Perhaps an argument over money, with Mr. Perkins taking the side of the lady of the house, got out of control.

"But the decorated hero of the Crimean War, although no longer so fresh or strong, didn't go without a fight, no matter how brief. You stayed out of sight for several weeks, Mr. Perkins. I believe that was because your face was visibly bruised in the brief fight where, no doubt to your horror, you killed the man that, I believe, you still regarded as a friend."

More tears came down one side of his face. "To this day," Perkins said quietly. "I love him like a brother to this day!"

"Quiet!" the lady of the house hissed.

"None of that now," McGann said. "Continue, Mr. Holmes."

"Supposedly, Mr. Perkins went off to London quietly one morning. Not long after that, Sir Earley began speaking unseen through oaken doors."

Real fear appeared on her face for the first time.

"But why did Mr. Perkins go to London at all? For it was he alone who left, Sir Earley being sadly dead, in an impulsive struggle that none of the three could have seen coming. Why? As I said, I believed he had to stay out of sight for several weeks for his bruised face to heal, but why did he have to risk leaving at all, and risk being seen leaving alone in the middle of the night?

"Fortunately, my friend Dr. Watson—who is eminently qualified to practice his profession, by the way, Mr. Perkins—helped me to test out the last bit of my theory. You see, I had wondered why it was that the animated, passionate orator whom I had read about was so singularly stiff and immobile in person." He strolled toward Perkins, who sat, gently sobbing, in his chair. All energy seemed to have left Lady Earley; she merely waited for the inevitable.

"I believe you were in London to see a doctor, yes, another real doctor, to treat an injury you had sustained in the brief fight, an injury so severe it could not be explained away, as there was no record of it ever happening to you. You who were in such perfect health, as you said in one of your more well-reported speeches."

Bryce Perkins looked up at Holmes, his face a hangdog expression of guilt. The entire left side of his face was wet. Holmes reached toward his face. "Please do not move, sir," Holmes said quietly, and Perkins obeyed.

Holmes grasped with thumb and forefinger, and with a brief effort, pulled a glass eye out of Bryce Perkins's right eye socket.

"You could not move around quickly, or be seen in good light," Holmes said. "Because glass eyes never quite match the natural colour of the remaining eye, nor do they move inside the socket. When Watson made a distracting noise, on my signal, you turned your neck, and the right eye remained frozen, as I suspected."

"We never meant to fall in love," Perkins said, between sobs. "We tried to be honourable about it. We made sure of privacy in one-half of the mansion so we could sit down and discuss it, like adults, with Barry. But his *temper*. He attacked me. When Viola hit him with that candlestick, he had already clawed my eye out and was going to start on the other one. He was strong, so strong. My friend was so strong!"

On the homeward train, Holmes was somewhat dejected. The case had given him the interesting twists and turns he craved. Now that it was over, I knew he would spend days angrily thumbing through the requests from suspicious husbands or suspicious wives or suspicious employers which made up the bulk of the cases he refused.

To jolly him out of his melancholy, I attempted to make conversation.

"I shall have to look up the poem in my little library when we get home."

Holmes would not have been Holmes if he had said, *What poem?* Of course, he replied: "*To Penshurst*, by Ben Jonson?"

"Yes?"

"You mean you can't remember it?"

"Some of us do not have your facility of memory, Holmes. I remember only that it was a tribute to the great estate of Penshurst, owned then by a patron of the poet, from which the town is named; I know the Robinette Manor was not the specific one, but still, one tries to breathe a bit of the arts to retain one's civilization."

"Well spoken, Watson. I remember a bit of it, from the middle, describing the estate's bounty. It goes thus."

And he recited, in rather good oratorical form:

"*To crown thy open table, doth provide*

"*The purpled pheasant with the speckled side;*

"*The painted partridge lies in every field,*

"*And for thy mess is willing to be killed.*"

And then, dropping out of recitation cadence, he said: "*Willing* to be killed? I somewhat doubt that. But willing or not, the painted partridge will be killed, Watson. To supply the table of the house's master ... or mistress."

THE SO-CALLED YOGA INSTRUCTOR

John Hearn

She was a resident here at Beemoor Village. Slightly older than me, I would guess. Mid-sixties probably. Nutty. Some kind of aging hippy with low-cut, long flowing dresses. Birkenstocks. No bra. Never a bra.

She called herself a yoga instructor because twice a week she sat with four or five other old hags, half of them in wheelchairs, straining to stretch an arm, theatrically inhaling and exhaling, tilting back their chests, shoulders and heads, then letting them cave in on themselves again and again as they nearly tumbled onto the ground. They reminded me of the inflatable balloon-like air dancers flailing around and folding in on themselves in tire center parking lots.

From my balcony, I could see their tiny circle out behind the community center, every Tuesday and Thursday at 11 a.m. With binoculars, I could clearly make out Joanne, the self-proclaimed yoga instructor, waiting until she had her "students" close their eyes before turning her own head this way and that, trying to catch a glimpse of whomever might be heading to the coffee bar or lining up for the shuttle bus to the mall. I mean are yoga instructors supposed to do that? Aren't they required to live by a code of honor and integrity? Isn't that what yoga is all about? Or am I thinking of Buddhism? Well, whether we're talking about yoga instructors or Buddhists, I'm pretty sure they are not supposed to be busybodies. Are they? Are they supposed to even care who is doing what with whom? Are they supposed to trick their students into believing that their teacher is meditating right along with them, intently transporting herself to a better, more serene place, eyes shut, when she's really peeking through a half-closed eyelid, wondering why Lisa Finkelbean is boarding the shuttle to Yang's Nail Salon rather than doing her yoga exercises? What kind of spiritual role model is that?

I know I sound sort of cold-hearted given that she was found dead just yesterday, and a bloody mess at that. And this kind of talk probably makes me a suspect, as well, seeing as how she was found dead and bloody in my bed.

Day 1

Detective Callahan was in his mid-forties, fit but not athletic, the kind of guy blessed with a rapid metabolism or the willpower to resist fast food and doughnuts, but not the motivation to regularly visit a gym. Under a full head of black hair were sloping, bushy brows and sad eyes that were echoed by a mouth drooping at the corners. In the middle of it all was a long, slightly bent, fairly narrow nose.

"Jack, how would you describe your relationship with the deceased?"

"Well ..."

"Is it okay if I call you 'Jack' or would you prefer 'Mr. McNamara'?"

"Jack is fine."

"How would you describe your relationship with the deceased, Jack?"

"We didn't really have a relationship, per se. By that I mean that we didn't interact regularly. We virtually didn't interact at all, except to maybe say hello when passing. That kind of thing."

"Where would you two 'pass' each other?"

"Oh, maybe in the coffee shop in the Community Center. Some place like that ... always here on the Beemoor grounds. Maybe by the pool. Maybe I saw her by the pool once."

"You never visited her in her apartment?"

"No."

"Never?"

"Detective, I'm not even sure where she lives. I mean I know she lives in Building 5, *Uplift!* but I'm not sure which unit she lives in ... or lived in, I guess you would say ... now."

"And she never stopped by here? Never stepped foot in your condo?"

"No, no, not once."

"Well, there was one time, at least," he said as he tilted his head toward my bedroom, now occupied by two crime scene investigators.

"Right. That's right. I guess she did come by—or was brought by—this one time. This one tragic time." I made a point of lowering and shaking my head slowly.

"*Brought* by? Do you know of anyone who would *bring* Ms. Barry to your place and then ... butcher her?"

"Whoever it was that killed her."

"Where were you last evening, Jack, between six and eight o'clock?"

"Playing shuffleboard."

Howie is my best friend in the Village, my only friend, really. We're close enough to just walk into each other's unlocked place without even knocking. He lives in unit 308, next door to mine, on the top floor here in Building 11, which is called *Affiliation!*. He's eighty-one, twenty years my senior, but still sharp, and funny too. He's a tall man, easily over six feet, which was probably rare back when he grew up. He might have been even taller a couple of decades ago. Investigator Callahan is over there talking to him now, likely asking a hundred questions about recent activity at my place, what he might have seen and heard, what he thinks about me, and whether I've ever said anything disparaging about that nutty so-called yoga instructor.

Howie is an astute guy, no doubt about it, but his brain weakens considerably by late afternoon and it's already early evening, so Callahan may get him to slip up. In fact, I think that's a given. It's just about this time every day that Howie's urinary problems act up, and they preoccupy him. He'll be wondering what he'll do if he has to relieve himself during the interview. Will it look suspicious? Will the exertion of pushing himself out of his recliner cause an accident? Will he make it to the bathroom on time? And that's when Callahan, who struck me as a seasoned interrogator, will slip in a comment like, "It's my understanding that Jack didn't care for Ms. Barry. Is that right?"

Big deal. So I didn't care for her. That means I murdered her? How many people in this retirement community don't care for me? Does that mean they'd deliberately kill me? Callahan himself doesn't like me, I can tell. Is he going to slaughter me? That's exactly what I'll ask him. When he gets around to telling me that Howie said I didn't care for the woman, I'll say, well you don't care for me, does that mean you're going to take my life? He'll probably come back with something like, well, you claimed that you didn't even know her, implying that you had no reason to not like her. That's when I'll come back and say, well, I believe that was more an inference on your part rather than an implication on mine, and I'll let him think about that for a few seconds, let him know who he's dealing with. In all likelihood, he doesn't interview many murder suspects who know the difference between 'implying' and 'inferring.' Maybe that will help him to see that I'm innocent. I've never known a murderer, not one, who has ever made that linguistic distinction, he'll think. Maybe this guy is blameless, after all, just an educated guy who had the misfortune of having a woman he barely knew and didn't care for—they'll be no denying that I didn't care for her, not now, I'm sure—get herself murdered in his bed. And then, after he's fully digested the significance of the imply/infer verb distinction, I'll add that I also didn't reveal my dislike for the poor woman because I didn't want to cast her in a bad light. That's just not my way, I'll tell him. That's not the kind of guy I am, one who would cast a dead woman in a bad light.

Day 2

According to the television news, the police do not have a suspect but are developing a person of interest. I'm sure by "person of interest" they mean "suspect." And I'm sure that's me. And by "developing", they mean, "harassing the shit out of." Callahan is acting like that Columbo character from the decades old television series, the persistent detective who acts sort of dumb, always popping up with one last question he forgot to ask the day before. That cigar chomping, trench coat wearing, fictional character wore a person down, drove him nuts, and then pounced. As far as I recall, he never lost a case.

I've decided the best thing for me to do is conduct my own investigation, and fast, before it's too late. Howie's helping me out and it's a good thing he is because my fellow Beemoor retirees want nothing to do with me. They're convinced I killed the yoga lady. I spent an hour in the coffee shop this morning hoping I could ask around, but the other customers pretended they didn't even see me. I said hello to one of the wheelchair-bound yoga students whose name I don't know, hoping to chat with her for a few minutes, but her face lit up with fright when she spotted me approaching and she quickly spun around and rolled away.

We've set up Howie's apartment as command central, mainly because mine has yet to be cleaned thoroughly, but also because Callalumbo keeps showing up, and I don't want him to know about my parallel investigation. We've been working our way through Beemoor's online residency list as well as its newsletter archives. From the former we downloaded pictures of our own persons of interest, including:

Jesus de Morales, *Affiliation!*'s maintenance guy. Rationale: he has access to all condos in this building. Jesus may be an illegal immigrant, but I can assure you that his possible status as a law-breaker, *ipso facto*, plays no role in my thinking. I'm not the kind of guy who despises illegal immigrants, not if they are hard working. (There's another term I'll work into my next conversation with Callalumbo. *Ipso facto. Ipso facto,* sir! is what I'll say at exactly the right moment. Something along those lines).

Sue Nelson, one of the "students" in Joanne's yoga "class." Rationale: there were many a day I focused my binoculars on Sue (she is not unattractive!) and could not help but notice a number of facial expressions suggesting disinterest and, I believe, dismay, or maybe even dislike. She is, though, wheelchair bound. Apparently. I say 'apparently' because I've witnessed wheelchair bound individuals who have suddenly jumped to their feet and raced to the front of the line on buffet night or to buy Michael Bublé tickets at the Beemoor theater's box office. Plus, Nelson is extremely broad shouldered, which means she may have sufficient upper-body strength to toss around a much smaller woman, even from a sitting position.

In a recent issue of the *Beemoor Village Voice,* Howie spotted a photograph of the deceased standing in close proximity to a young man. Identified as Buffalo orthodontist David Barry, Joanne's son, he was reported to have been visiting for a few days several months ago. Rationale: what kind of ungodly pressure must a parent impose upon a child to have him go through the torture required to enter and remain in the orthodontic profession? And what heinous retaliatory acts would that child, once an adult, be capable of committing?

Tony D'Angelo, a narcissistic know-it-all who was once a cop of some sort in a small North Jersey town. Tony lives at the other end of this building, on the first floor. He and I haven't gotten along since our public discussion about the nature of policing in American society. It took place last spring during my weekly Monday night shuffleboard tournament, during which he wore a seriously undersized t-shirt designed to show off whatever muscles he's developed through endless hours of weightlifting in our gym and, I suspect, through ingesting gallons of illicit human growth hormones. For more than a few minutes D'Angelo kept insisting that for twenty years he put his life on the line for his country. I kept saying that cops are overpaid and under worked, that they pad their overtime, have overly-generous, fat, unearned pensions which they collect after receiving years of phonied up disability payments, are often drunk or screwing some girl on the job, or both, and put their lives on the line with less frequency than a sixteen year old convenience store clerk. Rationale: see previous sentence.

We taped a picture of Joanne on Howie's living room wall and penned a big, black X over it. We then taped pictures of the suspects up there, two on each side of the deceased. Then we drank a couple of beers.

Howie was pretty much drunk after a beer and a half, so I finished his second one and sent him over to the Village Diner, which is what the Village Bean is called after four in the afternoon. The beer steadied his nerves but not his feet, so I helped him straddle his tricycle and pushed him off toward the eatery. In the trike's handlebar basket was an issue of the AARP magazine. I had glued a manila envelope to the back cover and placed a tiny mouse inside. When the pet store clerk asked me earlier that morning if my snake was about to be fed, I answered that a snake was about to be caught. "This mouse isn't a meal, it's bait."

Sue Nelson ate at the diner every late weekday afternoon. She had a cheese sandwich every Monday through Thursday and a fish fry on Friday. At least she did when I used to patronize the place, before my unpleasant dispute with Lou, the diner's unsanitary manager. When Howie arrived, Sue was sitting at a table with the ancient and nearly blind Gladys Sapperstein. He stopped and wished them a pleasant meal. As he did so, he surreptitiously dropped the mouse I had purchased that morning onto Sue's lap.

"Be sure to place your big paw on her shoulder as you drop the mouse," I recommended. "That way, if she does have feeling in her legs, if the wheelchair is a sick scam, she won't feel little Mickey when he falls onto her thighs."

Sitting at a nearby table and pretending to read the magazine, Howie carefully observed Sue's behavior. She remained unaware of the rodent until it reached the top of her blouse and tickled her neck. She thought she was scratching a random itch when she felt fur and then felt it move. On reflex, she swatted the mouse onto the table in front of her. When she realized what she had done, she screamed, pushed the table away so hard she sent cups and plates flying, rolled her chair backward forcibly, and, with help from her hefty upper torso, tipped it over, all while poor Sapperstein was trying to figure out what was going on. She did not pick herself up but remained motionless, on the floor, until the chair was righted and she was securely back in the saddle. Feeling guilty and ever the gentleman, Howie tried to help her up, but he couldn't bend over and was still unsteady on his feet from the beer, so he returned to command central, filled me in on the details, and we removed Sue Nelson from the suspect list.

Day 3

I woke up early and headed out to buy a couple of Dunkin' Donuts coffees at the plaza half a mile down the street. It wasn't even 7 a.m. when I closed the door behind me, turned toward the stairs leading to the parking lot, and bumped into Callahan. Literally. We were face-to-face. I was startled and pulled back a step.

"A little jumpy today, Jack?"

"I get that way when a guy appears unexpectedly from nowhere and is virtually on top of me. I mean your face was two inches from mine. What's that about?"

"Sorry. My mind was on something else."

"I'm on my way out, detective."

"Sure, sure. I do have one quick question for you though."

"What is it?"

"Well, I was talking to a couple of your neighbors yesterday who say they saw you entering Ms. Barry's apartment a few weeks ago."

"They saw me *entering* her apartment?"

"Her apartment *building*. They saw you walk up the stairs and approach her front door. Now, I thought you said you didn't even know which apartment was hers."

"Maybe it wasn't me they saw. Or maybe I *approached* her front door but didn't get all the way there. I could have turned and left. Or maybe I didn't know whose front door it was I approached ... allegedly."

"There are a lot of 'maybes' in that answer, Jack."

"You're presenting me with an extremely ambiguous scenario. There are, then, *ipso facto*, many 'maybes' involved."

"Maybe the details will come back to you during the day."

"Maybe."

So what if I did visit Joanne once? What does that prove? What if I dropped by after she had been bending over all afternoon by the pool, letting the top of her hippy dress fall open, exposing her breasts? What if the fabric caressed her nipples and had them as erect as a couple of tiny Marines at attention? What if she did all of this deliberately, while we chatted, and she flirted, hinting that she wouldn't mind spending some time with me? What if she practically invited me to come to her apartment, and then when I do, and with a bottle of wine, she doesn't even bother to come to the door, even though I knew she was home? And then when I ignored her the next day, she appears befuddled, as though she doesn't have a clue about what had upset me! And now, because *I* was treated uncivilly, I'm accused of being a murderer?

I got in the Jeep and picked up the coffee, but only after stopping at Walmart for a TracFone. When I returned, I prepped Howie on his upcoming call. After setting the phone to 'speaker,' I dialed the number and handed it to him.

"Hello, this is Barry Orthodontics, Erin speaking."

"Hi, Erin, this is Officer Tony D'Angelo. I'm calling from Beemoor Village here in South Florida. May I speak with Dr. Barry, please?"

"I'm sorry, but Dr. Barry isn't in today, sir."

"Oh?"

"Is this about his mother's … passing?"

"It is."

"I'm his wife, Officer D'Angelo, and I'd be happy to pass along any information you have."

"You know, Erin, I believe I met you and Dr. Barry a few days ago, when you two were visiting your mother-in-law. In fact, it was the day she … she passed."

"You must be mistaken. We haven't visited in about six months. In fact, David—that's my husband's name—was rushed to the hospital on that day—the day of his mother's death—for an emergency appendectomy. The very day his mom was … murdered. He's coming home from the hospital tomorrow."

"I must have been mistaken, Erin. Thanks very much for your time."

"But, what did …"

Howie hung up. And so we removed David Barry from the suspect list.

I hadn't noticed Jesus de Morales in the building since Joanne's death. Last evening I left a message with the maintenance office asking they send him to my unit to check the ceiling for a possible leak. As I left Howie's I found Jesus knocking on my door.

"Good morning, Jesus."

"Good morning, Jack. You have a problem with your ceiling?"

Jesus, in his early thirties, is a Guatemalan immigrant. He is good looking, short, and slightly overweight, but not soft. He's got the strength that moving all day, bending and lifting, gives a person. He doesn't wear a wedding ring. I once asked if he had kids and he said he did not. I would have expected a Catholic Guatemalan his age to have a wife and a few muchachos, and now wondered why he didn't. Did the young women in his neighborhood know of a flaw that made him unmarriageable? Did he have, say, anger issues? And how might his single status affect him psychologically, given that he is a part of such a family-oriented community? On this morning, he was wearing a long sleeve flannel shirt even though the temperature was already in the low eighties. The visor of his Marlins cap tilted downward a bit more than usual, obscuring his eyes somewhat.

I brought him into the bedroom. Almost half of the carpet had been removed, along with two large sections of drywall from behind where the bed had been, before the police removed that too.

"It's a mess, isn't it?" I prompted.

"It is."

"Have you heard about what happened here?"

"Yes."

"Did you know Ms. Barry at all?"

"I know only the people in this building." He looked at the ceiling, searching, in what I thought was an exaggerated manner, for signs of a leak.

"I don't actually have a leak, Jesus. I need the carpet and dry wall replaced and thought maybe you could do it for me. I mentioned the leak so your boss wouldn't get suspicious and think you were doing private work. I know roof work is paid for by the association."

"I can't help you, Jack. Doing private work for tenants is against the rules. I could lose my job."

"It'll be off the books, under the table. I won't tell a soul and will make it worth your while."

"I'd like to help you but ... you know ... I need this job. Sorry."

I knew he wouldn't lose his job and that he had done similar off-the-books work for many others, and not just in this building.

"Okay, I thought I'd ask." As I held out my hand to shake his, I added, "No hard feelings."

It was then that I noticed a pronounced scratch distending from under the cuff of his flannel shirt. It was on his right wrist and was covered with what looked like a woman's facial make-up.

"Ouch!" I exclaimed as I stared at the scrape.

His eyes followed mine. "Thorns. The damned bushes out back."

As Jesus opened the door to leave, Callalumbo was standing there. Surprised, Jesus took a quick half-step back into the tiny kitchen and emitted a soft whimper.

"Are you Jesus de Morales?"

"Yes, sir."

"I'm Detective Callahan. I've been trying to get in touch with you."

"I've been home, sick for a couple of days."

"I'd like to talk to you, in about an hour. Be at the maintenance office."

"Okay."

Jesus left and Callahan walked into my apartment.

"Come in, Detective," I said after he had already taken the three strides that brought him through the kitchen, into the living room, and to the door where he gazed into my demolished bedroom.

"We have a problem, Jack."

"*We?*"

"I think so. I just got off the phone with David Barry, the deceased's son."

"Oh?" 'Already,' I thought. Howie had hung up the phone less than an hour ago.

"Seems his wife got a call from someone who referred to himself as Officer Tony D'Angelo. He was asking questions about her husband's whereabouts on the day of the murder."

"I didn't know Tony was still an active police officer."

"He's not."

"Impersonating a police officer. That sounds like a serious offense."

"It is. But I don't think it's D'Angelo who's guilty of it."

"Really?"

"Really."

"Cops don't commit crimes?"

"Knock off the shit, McNamara." Callahan shook his head for emphasis and waited a few seconds before continuing. "You do know D'Angelo, right?"

"It'd be more accurate to say that I know of him. I've actually had very little to do with him."

"Like you didn't really know Joanne Barry?"

"Exactly."

"So you don't really know him. Does that mean you don't care for him, either? Is there anyone in this complex you do get along with?"

"I get along with Howie, the guy next door."

"Speaking of your friend, Mr. Barry's wife says the guy who harassed her sounded like an elderly gentleman."

I walked Callahan to the door and watched him descend the stairs. Rather than continue on to his vehicle, he turned left. I leaned toward the railing along the edge of the third floor landing and kept watching as he made his way to the end of the building where he knocked on D'Angelo's door. I grabbed a beer and brought a kitchen chair back to the door which I had left cracked open a few inches. Twenty minutes later both men stepped out into the sunshine and shook hands, as you'd expect fellow cops to do. D'Angelo was wearing a sleeveless t-shirt and the long, baggy shorts that kids wear. His bronze skin was oiled up, glistening in the sunlight. Callahan headed back toward his car and I closed the door.

I drove to Taco Bell and bought four chicken Chalupa Supremes. I knew Howie wouldn't eat two of them, but I was concerned that if I gave him only one, I'd be reminding him that he'd be leaving this world soon. I got you only one chalupa, Howie, because you don't eat much anymore. It's not like the old days when you would probably have put away four of these damned things. Five, maybe. Well, that's not me. I don't do things that way. Let the Jesus de Morales and Tony D'Angelos of this world mistreat our elderly. Do you think guys like that give a shit about some dying old man—and a war vet, yet!—when they go around murdering an apparently innocent woman, and on some blameless guy's bed? That's not how I operate. I'm the kind of human being who will give Howie two Chalupa Supremes, the same number I have, and let him maintain a shred of dignity by hiding one in the bag along with the wrapper of the one he did eat and the napkins too and twisting up the whole shebang like it was only paper refuse waiting to be dropped into the trash can.

The local news came on as we were eating. A reporter stood in the parking lot in front of this section of *Affiliation!* I walked to the window and saw her back as she faced the camera. She claimed that her police sources told her they were zeroing in on a suspect and hoped to have their investigation completed soon. As she was signing off, the camera panned up to my door. I pressed the 'off' button on the remote. Howie and I discussed the relative merits of de Morales and D'Angelo as our primary suspect. Neither one of us was sure who was more likely to have committed such an unspeakable atrocity. After a few minutes, Howie had to pee and figured if he was going to go through the effort of extricating himself from the recliner, he might as well stay up and walk from the toilet to his bed and take a nap.

I returned to my apartment, sat on my back balcony, sipped a Jameson, and ran every scenario I could think of through my head.

And that's when I saw D'Angelo. The sun had set but night hadn't fallen. Darkness filled the woods behind *Affiliation!* but there were various shades of grey settling between the building and the tree line. D'Angelo was wearing black pants and a grey t-shirt. He was carrying a black plastic trash bag. It wasn't full, like most bags are when they're removed from the house and about to be tossed, and he wasn't holding it at its top, letting the bag hang free. It was wrapped tightly around its content and clutched under his right arm—which was away from the building but partially visible as he approached the woods.

I quietly dropped from the chair to my knees, moving slightly to my left; behind a folding room partition I use to block the direct sunlight. I brought the binoculars to my eyes and through the crack between two of the panels, watched as his head swiveled slowly in both directions as he walked toward a never-used, overgrown pathway. I focused on his left hand. It looked like he was wearing a latex glove. I guessed he wore one on his other hand, which I couldn't see. He stepped onto the path and as he was disappearing I noticed what looked like a stick or a handle, six or eight inches long, protruding up from his rear pocket. And then he was gone.

An hour passed and darkness fell. I barely moved, still behind the partition but sitting now, waiting, staring at the black wall of vegetation, my eyes regularly darting back to the path. After an hour, D'Angelo appeared, hesitated at the tree line, looked both ways, and walked toward his condo. I stood, stepped over to the railing and leaned out to visually follow him home. But he didn't go home. Instead, he walked to the end of the building and out toward the parking lot. I hurried through my living room and kitchen, opened my front door, stood behind a pillar and saw D'Angelo walk to dumpster, open its door, reach behind him, remove the object from his back pocket, and drop it in.

My heart was racing. I wanted to call Callahan but didn't trust him. I fought the urge to wake up Howie to run this suspicious activity by him, but instead returned to the back balcony to try to make sense of it all.

Hours later, before the sky had begun to lighten, I grabbed my flashlight and left. I quietly opened Howie's unlocked door, took a step into his kitchen, and reached over to the counter where he kept his EZ Grabber. Two minutes later, I slid the dumpster's door open and pointed the light inside. A couple of rats quickly disappeared, one grazing my cheek as it leapt from the big green box, causing the flashlight to fall onto a pile of trash bags. I leaned as far into the smelly container as I could and with my outstretched arm reached for the flashlight. It was only an inch from my fingers but I couldn't extend myself further. I tugged at the white trash bag on which the flashlight sat and gently pulled it toward me. My fingertips grazed the red plastic cylinder, causing it to roll farther away from me. Before hearing it hit the steel floor, I noticed its light catch a shiny object a foot or so away. I couldn't see what it was, but knew I had to find out. I poked around the trash bags with the EZ Grabber, grasped the metal object, silver and curved, and pulled it from the dumpster. A garden trowel, its handle resembling what I saw jutting up from D'Angelo's back pocket.

I felt dizzy as I kept the Grabber's suction tipped tongs tight against the scoop-shaped blade and walked home where I deposited it into a Glad freezer bag. As I finally exhaled, the rising sun reminded me that I hadn't slept in a day.

DAY 4

I entered Howie's with two extra-large Dunkin' Donuts coffees and a shovel I rented a few minutes earlier from Tooland. I had a feeling we'd need the caffeine. I knew we'd need the shovel. Our plan was to position Howie on his back balcony with the TracFone. At the first sign that D'Angelo was about to enter the woods to check out the safety of his hiding place, he would give me call.

Not wanting to risk D'Angelo seeing me, I entered the woods fifty yards or so down the tree line from our building. Twenty feet in, I walked back toward the path he had taken, and scanned the ground for a sign that a patch of it had been overturned, a hole had been dug, evidence of murder buried.

I let my feet and my eyes take me where they thought the stash was buried. The former left the path every ten yards or so, as the latter shifted from one side of the narrow trail to the other. After four or five minutes, I realized that I was paying more attention to the vegetation than the ground. I had stared at this wooded area from my balcony a thousand times, but had I been asked to describe a single plant within it, would not have been able to do so. It was all just a variegated green backdrop. Now, with them, brushing against them, smelling them, it was different. Like the difference between staring at a shelf of beer bottles until you don't see them anymore, and drinking a freshly poured craft brew. Sort of. There were bushes, twenty feet tall and as wide, with puffy yellow flowers and what looked like rows of stubby pine needles and green branches that resembled frozen praying mantises trying to blend in. There were tall, wide trees with leaves that looked like those on the maple tree behind the Massachusetts house I grew up in, but this smaller variation contained a generous smattering of reddish flowers. There were bright green ferns, tall and thick and surrounded by plumes of palm leaves. It struck me that this vegetation experience could conceivably be as intoxicating as my regular beer experience, and I promised myself that I'd spend more time outside, in nature, and less on my concrete balcony— assuming I stayed out of prison and had the freedom to do so.

Before realizing it, I was at the far end of the wooded area, staring at a street of worn out 1950s houses, square or rectangular, faded stucco, with garages that had become third bedrooms, rusted room air conditioners stuck to outer walls like blemishes, each residence a few feet from the next. From a narrow, weedy median running down the middle of the street stood a six foot tall metal fence post at the top of which sat a crooked wooden turquoise sign that read, in pink lettering, *Sunshine Cove.* I had thought the condo golf course, where old Beemoor men and women shared a social ritual around which they organized their dying days, extended this far down on this south side of the woods. But far from being a place where life-long dreams were played out on chemically maintained fairways, the area was a dream graveyard, steeped in the decaying scent of relative impoverishment. I began to wonder if maybe a struggling, angry resident of *Sunshine Cove* was responsible for Joanne's murder. And maybe D'Angelo's woodland adventure was something other than what it seemed. I suddenly wondered where Jesus lived. I turned and began to retrace my steps when I saw it.

Just a few feet from the leafy pathway, in the middle of a wide patch of sand, sat a mound of potting soil-like muck. I turned over a shovel full and then a second and saw black plastic. I reached down and pulled up the bag. I opened the top of the bag and saw clothing. Bloody clothing. I opened it wider and saw a long bladed knife. I tightened the bag's blue ties and headed back to *Affiliation!*

My heart was racing but my head slowed for the first time since the murder. I was overwhelmed by a sense of having the freedom to relax, and not just today when this taint of criminality was sticking to me like sweat, but from this day forward. Maybe I'd escape a prison sentence and get to enjoy Florida's flora after all. And what about its fauna? I mean dolphins surround this state, don't they? And everyone's always yapping about wanting to swim with them. It's become a high priority "must-do" on every old person's "bucket list." Then it occurred to me that I should drop the "flora and fauna" phrase on Callahan when I dump my bag full of evidence on his desk. I'll say something like, I'm glad I could help you out, Detective, but cannot do so in the future, as I will be busy during the next several years immersing myself in the state's flora and fauna. That phrase will give him the opportunity to take in the full measure of Jack McNamara. My mind jumped again and I was visualizing a carefree, in-the-moment life, with the plants and the dolphins, when I saw the expanse of green grass and *Affiliation!s* beige stucco through the trees.

I picked up my pace, held the bag to my chest with both arms, stepped onto the open back lawn, and caught the quickest glimpse of a furious-looking Tony D'Angelo. He resembled a bull. Charging me. He threw himself into my midsection and we both fell to the ground, the plastic trash bag between us. I felt the breath being knocked out of me, and heard it streaming from D'Angelo's chest too, like air being released from a compressor. The heavy former cop rolled off me and onto his back, and the bag went with him, stuck to his chest.

That's when I noticed Callahan, directly in front of me, extending a hand, and pulling me onto my feet. I looked down and saw the blood pouring from D'Angelo's chest, where his knife, still in the bag, was lodged. I tried hard to breathe, then looked up at Howie's balcony where he stood at the rail and returned his wave.

Day 5

After sleeping on the sofa most of the day, I was now, at dusk, sipping a beer on the balcony with a freezer bag of ice on my upper chest and my arm in a sling. The woods had blurred into an invisible backdrop hours earlier. The doctor recommended Advil for my broken clavicle, but I opted for a couple of Southern Tier IPAs instead. The effect was similar but the smell and taste of the beer carried, as they always did, memories of camaraderie and meaning, of things and people greater than and outside of me, of times gone by.

Callahan had stopped by earlier to fill me in on new details. New, at least to me. For one thing, D'Angelo was dead. For another, he had been seeing Joanne. Not seeing her, really, but meeting up to have sex, something D'Angelo apparently was doing with several Beemoor residents. When Joanne realized there wasn't a future with this guy, she began to look around. Specifically, she looked at me. D'Angelo was in her apartment on the evening I stopped by with the wine, assumed it was a scheduled get-together, and became furious with her. And me. He stewed for weeks. And plotted. Then lured Joanne into my apartment on a Monday night, when he knew I'd be playing shuffleboard and my door would be unlocked. Callahan read all of this in Joanne's diary, right up to last Monday night, when she had put on one of her hippy dresses and headed over to 307 *Affiliation!* The journal was discovered in her refrigerator's vegetable crisper only a day ago.

Drowsy, again, I debated going back to the couch for another nap, when my eye was drawn to movement by the woods. A male wearing a backpack and carrying a small Styrofoam cooler was stepping onto the narrow path leading to *Sunshine Cove*. It was Jesus.

☞

THE MECHANICAL DETECTIVE

John Longenbaugh

It was a raw April afternoon in 1889, the rain on the window pane streaked pea-soup yellow from the morning's fog, and I was sitting in the parlor that I shared with Ponder Wright, the man known throughout London as the Mechanical Detective. He was reading a copy of the Times and I sat across from him, staring idly at my empty glass, half-asleep from the ennui of the weather and a day empty of employment. Abruptly my friend spoke, his voice carrying that odd undertone of metallic echo from the copper plating of his chin and upper larynx.

"The measurements are one point eight grams of sodium bicarbonate, and slightly less, one point six four, of tartaric acid. Both powders are located in the top left drawer of my laboratory desk." He then turned a page of the paper, sending it and the sleeve of the red silk dressing gown he wore this afternoon fluttering. "And mind you measure them out precisely."

I stared at him in astonishment. As his friend and mechanic, I believed I had a fair overview of Ponder Wright's myriad abilities. Yet till now I had not been aware that he could read minds.

"What? Why?"

"Because, my dear Danvers, the gasogene that you purchased last Tuesday, which I deemed a silly frivolity, requires those two chemicals to operate."

"And how did you know I was thinking of filling and operating the gasogene?" Wright lowered his copy of the Times and looked at me, his blue left eye merry and the lens of his right eye glowing an ember red from within the copper plating of the right side of his face.

"A simple deduction. You were looking at your glass, wondering if it was yet time for either gin or whiskey, either of which would be greatly augmented by a splash of tonic or soda water. Since yesterday afternoon we've lacked both, which as I recall was your rationale for purchasing the gasogene in the first place."

The Cockney salesman who sold me this intriguing contraption ("quite the item among the fashionable Consulting Detective set, I assure you sir") had not supplied me with an instruction manual, and with little knowledge of chemistry I left the device on the sideboard for future contemplation.

I crossed to it now and unscrewed the top of the two glass globes, then turned to Wright's laboratory table and removed the appropriate envelopes of powder. "You'll want to fill the bottom chamber with the powders, and then put water in the upper one," Wright said, as he took another of his abominable herbal lozenges from the bowl at his side.

"I don't recall asking for your assistance," I said, measuring the powders.

"You did not," he agreed. "But seeing as even the prescribed chemicals in improper amounts have been known to cause gasogenes to explode, my assistance contributes to both your physical health and the safety of our living quarters."

It was still early enough in our acquaintance for me to find his behavior annoying. Three months prior I had responded to his advertisement for a mechanic surgeon in an attempt to supplement my paltry military pension. I performed maintenance on his prosthetics through the morning, stayed for a tea which turned into a dinner, and we parted late that evening as friends. The next week when I dropped by for a visit he suggested I move in as a flatmate, paying a reduced rent if I agreed to be his on-call mechanic. Since my own lodgings were both dear and geographically disadvantaged, I agreed, and so for the last three months we had enjoyed a relatively pleasant co-habitation of his spacious and centrally located flat on Clacker Street.

Now we lived companionably enough, him pursuing his vocation and me at least dabbling in mine. While I still took on the occasional case, I had seen enough of wounded and dying men with the Royal Steam Artillery, enough blood and rust, to last a lifetime. So I chiefly followed my art by maintaining the delicate machinery of Wright's prosthetics—both legs, his right arm, and the right hemisphere of his face which included an automatonic ear (a devil to calibrate) and an automatonic eye, supplied with a number of specialized lenses. Though the eye was lidless with an opaque lens, and the brow merely painted on to the brass plate, my friend was capable of a remarkable amount of expression with it. I would swear at times I saw it wink.

As I filled the second globe with water, he shook the paper and gave a snorting laugh. "Another triumph for the Great Detective, I see." Like many brilliant men Wright had more than a fair share of vanity, and it galled him to see the successes of his rivals.

"So I have heard!" I agreed. "It's been quite the year for him. Would that you attracted as many cases." The Great Detective had been the subject of a series of highly popular, if somewhat fictionalized, stories in *The Strand* magazine, and now was apparently batting clients away with a stick—or perhaps a violin.

Wright shrugged, with a slight squeak. "His success is as much due to his biographer's literary skills as his own abilities," he said. "I'm sure he's nowhere near as clever as Whatshisnoodle claims. Perhaps you should try your hand at writing up some of my cases."

I laughed, though secretly pleased by the thought. "I'm a mechanic, not an author. Besides, this month you've seen some brisk business from the Yard."

"Me and a dozen other 'Consulting Detectives,' you mean," he said with a sigh. "It's a buyer's market, Danvers. Every week carries the story of a police case solved thanks to the assistance of some crime-solving expert or another. It is fortunate I am 'mechanical,' otherwise how would I stand out in such a glutted field?"

This was true. Since the first appearance of the Great Detective in London just eight years prior, there had been an increasing number of rivals to his fame and fortune. There were doctors, lawyers, and journalists who'd all taken up consulting detective work. And Wright, despite his unusual appearance and mechanical augmentation, was far from the most unusual. There was also a blind detective, and an Indian Raj, and an unkempt elderly man who solved his crimes never leaving the table at his favorite restaurant. There were priests and chemists and foppish young aristocrats. There were even female detectives, though I have always found it difficult to believe that the fair sex is capable of rational analysis of anything.

"To be but one of a roster of consultants leaves me far too idle," he continued, as I shot seltzer into my glass, and regrettably outside of it as well. "And I do not do well with idleness."

"It's a good thing then that the growth in consulting detectives has been matched by an equivalent increase in criminal activity."

"Nonsense," he replied, waving his silk-sleeved right arm at me dismissively with a remarkably life-like motion. "Society has ever been a complex web of criminal activity at all levels. The press is simply reporting it more often. A suitable amount of violence and mayhem is a wonderful way to sell newspapers, not to mention kineographs." His gaze swept down the page in front of him, filled with reports of foreign affairs in the far-flung outposts of the Empire.

"But what of the great crimes, Danvers? What of the syndicates, corporations and other financial institutions that profit from human misery? What of the misdeeds and injustices perpetrated in other lands in our name, blighting our Imperial sun?"

He was prone to these sorts of rants on occasion, and I lost no time in nipping it in the bud. "Now now, no more of that sort of thing, Wright. There are times I swear you're going positively Anarchist on me."

He looked at me steadily for a moment with that unnerving placidity of which he was capable, his flesh as still as the metal that mirrored it. Then he threw his head back and gave a very human laugh. "Never fear, Danvers. Though parts of my body were manufactured by a variety of European craftsmen, my heart," and he tapped his chest, "is resolutely British."

Bobby, Mrs. Vassar's boy, knocked at the door. "Begging your pardon sirs, but there's a message come from Scotland Yard for Mr. Wright, and a hackney wot's come with it." I rose and took the letter, handing the boy sixpence, which he pocketed with a street arab's dexterity before vanishing down the stairs. Wright gave me a nod to read it.

"It's a job, Wright. The Yard wants you to come in and assist with a series of interrogations."

"Interrogations?"

"Yes. It says that it's with regards to a murder."

Wright frowned. "Fractionally more interesting. But why interrogations? Why offer me work which does not allow the fullest range of my talents?"

Wright had talked himself out of work he considered beneath his talents before, but our larder was bare and I was having none of it. "Perhaps this will spark your interest. The interrogation is of a series of experimental automatons."

Wright smiled. "That *is* good news indeed. In crime, novelty is invariably good news." With that inhuman rapidity of which he was on occasion capable, he stood and crossed the room to the coat rack in a flash, the red silk dressing gown hanging in the air for a moment before drifting to the floor. "Now, why don't you grab one of my extra arms for the trip? I would recommend the Tool Kit." As I left for the shop to retrieve it, he called after me, "And do make sure the gasogene is well out of the sunlight."

Outside on Clacker Street the steam hackney from the Yard awaited us, a dark-plated and smudged monstrosity whose looming stack belched a gray plume. With a nod to the driver we climbed inside and with a loud collection of creaks from pistons and gears we were off.

After we settled in I yelled to Wright, "I'll say this for a steam hackney—it's a smoother ride than your traditional carriage."

"If a damn sight louder," he yelled back. "I prefer the horse-drawn version, with its quiet and significantly lower rate of explosion."

This was true—no less than a dozen steam hackneys had exploded on London streets within the last six months, of differing model and manufacture, and while there was an Official Enquiry into each case, with grieving widows and children receiving substantial compensation, the general belief among the Mechs with whom I raised a glass was that the contrivances were poorly-built, erratically maintained and incompetently operated.

Still, ours rolled along the street in a pleasant enough fashion, cushioned from the worst of the cobblestones by the innovation of rubber-rimmed tires. Since conversation was difficult, I settled across from my friend and regarded him, while he returned to reading his paper.

The surgeons who operated on Wright had been not just skilled doctors but true artists. The copper plate that covered the right side of his face from temple to chin did not mirror the left side, but was instead a bold and burnished creation whose seams were chased by a trail of tiny silver rivets. The eye socket was inset with a delicate gold casing, and the eye itself, capable of interchanging a variety of lenses of different hue and magnification, was as fine a piece of machinery as I've ever seen.

"I have the best face my brother could buy," Wright was fond of saying, and it was true: His brother Mordecai was both a rich and powerful man. When Ponder suffered his injuries his brother made sure that he had the most skilled medical treatment possible, not only saving his life but providing prosthetics of a quality exceeding any I had ever seen.

Perhaps no other man in the Empire could have done so. Mordecai's extensive collection of duties and allegiances stretched across a variety of Her Majesty's bureaucracies. He was an advisor to the Science Corps, a fellow in the Royal Academy of Surgeons, a liaison to both the Foreign and Patent Offices, and was rumored to be a player in the "Secret Service," the branch of government necessary for the maintenance and security of the Empire. Certainly in the short time I had known Ponder, his brother had called in his filial debt no less than three different times, and while my friend resented this, there was little he could do. "I daresay my soul is my own, but far too much of the rest of me is merely leased from Mordecai," he said on one occasion.

With a clatter and final burst of steam we arrived in front of Metropolitan Police Headquarters. Wright instructed me to tip the driver and I did, though grumbling at paying for an official conveyance. This I have learned regarding those born to luxury: they can be an expensive nuisance to those living with them in poverty.

I followed Wright through the door and down to the office of Inspector Garrison, an open-faced and pleasant fellow who had been our liaison on several occasions in the past. He rose to meet us from his desk.

"Ah! Wright! Danvers. Thanks for your speed, gentlemen. May I introduce you to Brigadier Farnsworth?" At this he nodded to a gentleman wearing the coat of an army officer standing in the corner. I saluted reflexively, but Wright gave only a small nod.

"Gentlemen. Pleased to meet you both," Farnsworth said. His pale but weary face, as well as the florid color of his cheeks and nose, marked him for a desk officer, not a campaigner. He extended his hand and I shook it, and then he turned to Wright. With the sound of tiny well-oiled gears Wright's right arm rose and extended his hand towards the Brigadier, who placed his hand somewhat hesitantly on its upraised fingers. They closed and he performed the everyday but astonishingly complex task of shaking hands.

"Remarkable," Farnsworth said in a low tone as the hand released his. "I, that is, apologies if it's an awkward subject. ..."

"Not at all, Brigadier," said Wright. "I confess I am amazed each and every day what my body can accomplish with such delicate skill. Of course, it is no less amazing what my left arm can do as well, but we are inured, are we not, to the familiar miracles of the flesh?" He raised his right hand up before his face and turned it back and forth. "'What a piece of work is Man,' says the Bard, and I say what a piece of work has Man constructed, such intricate and delicate machinery that can mimic the very form and purpose of that wrought by his Creator. What does it mean for us to stand on the cusp of rivaling His power with so little of His purported wisdom?" He smiled. "But we are not here to effuse poetry or theology. We are here to solve a crime."

"Just so. Now as to the details ..." Garrison began.

"I assume they involve an Inventor under contract to create the world's first killing automaton," interrupted Wright.

The Brigadier looked startled and shot a glance at Garrison, who shook his head. "Not a word from me, sir." They both looked at my friend.

"Oh come, gentlemen. A murdered man, a collection of automatons to interrogate and inspect, and a senior representative from Her Majesty's Army. It is no great feat of ratiocination to conclude the broad outline." He took a seat and we all did the same. "But now: the details?"

The Brigadier pulled on the tips of his graying moustache before answering. "Firstly, Mr. Wright, I do not affirm that the professor's work for his Country had anything to do with the hypothetical project to which you refer. According to the details of the Crimean Accord, there is a ban on the research, development and deployment of automatons designed for lethal purpose in warfare. And though certain foreign powers are reputedly in violation of the Accord, Her Majesty's Government has not sanctioned any such behavior."

"Now, all that being said ..." began Wright.

"All that being said. We did have a contract with Professor Thaddeus Quire, the celebrated inventor, for a certain automata design that could be used, purely in an ancillary matter, on the field of battle. Carrying supplies, ferrying medical equipment, that sort of thing."

"That sort of thing," said Wright, his voice neutral. Still, the Brigadier stopped and stared at him for a moment, trying to detect irony.

"Yes. In any case, he had been reporting significant progress with his assignment and said that he would have a prototype for our inspection ready to be delivered by the end of the month, assuming that he was able to complete some other outstanding contracts. This morning the professor was discovered in his basement laboratory, dead. In the lab with him were three complete automatons. We believe that one of them, very possibly the prototype that he was developing, was his murderer."

"Was the professor working for the military exclusively?" I asked.

Garrison shook his head. "Professor Quire was a highly-regarded inventor of not just automatons but a whole host of other devices. He had an exclusive contact with Harrods—perhaps you've seen his service mannequins?"

"I have!" I volunteered, and when the men turned to me, I explained. "They not only exhibit to customers the latest fashions, but assist them in donning these clothes in private dressing rooms. Many of the fairer sex prefer their assistance to that of shop girls, or so I have been told."

"Preserving the modesty of the Empire's women as they shop. A noble achievement indeed!" said Wright. He turned back to the Inspector. "And what makes you believe that his death was caused by an automaton and not accident or a human agent?"

"Firstly," said Garrison, "the nature of his injuries. Death occurred from a savage set of beatings on the head and body, as from repeated blows from a heavy metal object. Secondly, the location of the body, which was found at the top of the stairs that lead down to the laboratory, means that it must have been carried to its position. Bloodstains halfway up the stairs and on the landing, where the body lay, confirm this, and that the initial attack occurred halfway up the stairs. Thirdly, the Brigadier's assertion that one of these automatons, though we don't know which, was capable of killing a man. And fourthly, because the door to the professor's basement laboratory was locked from the inside, with the key still inside the lock."

Wright gave a short barking laugh. "Capital! A murder inside a hermetically sealed chamber! Inspector, my thanks! I have been waiting my entire career for a classic locked room mystery!"

"Look here, Mr. Wright. This is a serious matter," said the Brigadier. "I was told that you were the man best suited for this job. If you're not, I have no doubt that the Inspector could find another specialist. ..."

Wright raised his human hand. "Please excuse any lack of decorum in expressing my enthusiasm, Brigadier. You must understand: my brain is built to solve puzzles, and to hear that this is not only a murder but a mystery is welcome news indeed. Now, where are the suspected automatons currently stored?"

"We've brought them here to the station, Wright," said Garrison, relieved to reassert some official authority. "Though not without effort. Took a dozen of my men all morning to move the three of them." With that he crossed to the door and motioned for us both to follow him.

We went down another corridor to a small interrogation room with a long wooden table in its center. Standing at the opposite wall approximately six feet apart from each other were a trio of standing automatons, each roughly human size. The first was bulky and boxy, with a thick steel chest essentially rectangular and legs resembling segmented pipes, while the second machine was tall and elegant, with a torso of shining brass and a turret-like neck. The third was markedly feminine in form, with a buxom chest, curved abdomen and flared hips, not to mention remarkably shapely legs. Each face sported eyes, mouths and ears, but only the "female" automaton featured a visage with any significant detail. In fact a remarkable amount of artistic attention had been spent on lips that looked positively inviting, and alone of the three figures she sported colored glass eyes, of a light emerald hue.

"Ah!" said Wright happily. "And these are our suspects?"

"The only three of the professor's automatons that were complete."

"There were others deemed incapable of independent movement or operation? According to whom?"

Garrison shook his head. "Believe me, Wright, there wasn't another object in the room capable of independent movement. His lab tables were covered by heaps of assorted pieces of machinery, but these were the only automatons near completion, and for that matter the only ones connected to aetheric batteries."

Wright examined the trio more closely. "I see that they are inactive. Were they in this state when discovered in the lab?"

"Each was motionless, yet their service switches were set to on. All three had batteries that were at least half-full. For safety's sake we deactivated them before moving."

"Well, we shall at least begin here." Wright turned to Garrison and the Brigadier. "Now, gentlemen, I shall begin my interrogation. My natural empathy with machines requires my full concentration and absolutely no distractions. I will ask you both to leave, while Danvers here stands by ready to assist. As soon as we finish our interrogation we will return to your office." Garrison nodded and despite a mildly protesting look from the Brigadier the two men left the room without comment.

"Now let's see what we have," Wright said, giving a rap to the face of the first of the three automatons, then bending down to examine its right hand, whose fingers were curled into a fist. "Danvers, have you brought your tool kit? We might have to get into the code panels on this thing."

"Code panels?" I asked, opening up my valise to reveal my collection of wrenches, screwdrivers, pistons and parts. "Wright, I'm a mecha-surgeon, not a Maker. You'll have to explain that to me."

He smiled. "You are such a dab hand with the oil can and the spanners that it is easy for me to forget you've no real experience with how automatons 'think.' Very well. You should know if you don't already that one cannot 'interrogate' an automaton. They are machines incapable of free will or intent, and therefore of conscious deception. Lying is impossible for them. But you can examine them like any machine, with the fortunate addition of being able to determine its operating code."

"And code is ..."

"You understand how an analytical engine operates, do you not? A series of punches are made onto a card which is then 'read' by the shuttle of the machine itself. Automatons like these, with highly advanced analytical engines, are capable of independent action and following simple commands, but their capabilities are defined by their code cards. Just as an Orthodox Jew may not light a match on the Sabbath or a practicing Catholic eat any meat but fish on Fridays, each automaton is defined by its own code of behavior."

"You intend to ask these automatons about their religious beliefs?"

"They have no beliefs," he said with a scornful laugh. "One might as well ask a washboard or a loom what its belief is. But the code each carries defines the scope of its prescribed actions. An automaton is simply not capable of carrying out an action which has not been defined by its code."

With that he activated with a triumphant flick of his human wrist a switch located under the left shoulder of the first automaton. As it hummed to life, he continued. "Now, before we take the rather more drastic step of opening up their analytical engines to discover any discrepancies, we can make a preliminary survey of what tasks each machine is capable of simply by asking them a series of questions." He turned back to the blocky figure. "Automaton, what is your name?"

"Hector." It spoke with that grating rumble common of the more menial automatons, those providing brute labor such as construction and moving freight.

"Good afternoon Hector. And what is your purpose?" The automaton was silent. Wright turned to me. "Ah. It is clear that Hector's code is incomplete. Automatons that are capable of speech and fully coded will always answer that question when asked. Very well then." He walked around to the other side of the table from Hector, motioning me to join him. "Hector: exhibit mode. Execute any presentational tasks."

Hector began marching in place, his inhumanly thick legs tramping the floor with such force that we felt each thump.

Wright smiled. "Astonishing, isn't it? Every time I see a walking automaton, even one as rudimentary as Hector here, I am amazed by the degree of craftsmanship required. There are over two hundred and fifty individual muscles in the legs of a human being, and all of them are involved in the everyday process of walking across a room. Learning to use my prosthetics was at times such a frustrating enterprise that I wonder how I ever managed my original limbs."

After a few seconds Hector stopped, then as if turned contortionist bent forward from the trunk and planted its arms on the ground, transforming itself into a sort of table. It then began again to shuffle on its now four legs. "Remarkable. Evidently Hector can also serve as a mechanical pallet," said Wright. At that moment Hector's arms began to lengthen, and from both his left and right sides metal flanges began to expand outwards. At the same time, his feet produced thick rubber tires. After a moment he tipped forward seventy degrees, and we were facing a wheeled and slowly advancing metal shield large enough for two men. "Stop," said Wright, and Hector did.

"Thus far it seems that our professor, in designing his automaton, stayed well within the Crimean protocol," said Wright. "Hector's primary purposes, as advertised, seem to be to convey supplies and provide protection on the battlefield from an enemy fusillade. But let us see what other skills he has in his codebook." He turned back to the machine: "Hector: continue with exhibition mode."

For the next ten minutes the blocky automaton cycled through its prescribed actions, producing a medical kit, emitting a loud klaxon, and transforming into a small armored sleeping shelter. Finally at the end of the demonstration he stood before us, as blocky and unthreatening as a ladder. Wright said, "Display all devices that could be hazardous to a human being."

Hector extended its right hand and lifted its thumb. With a flinty spark it produced a small flame, just fierce enough to light a cheroot.

"Hector is not our killer," said Wright.

"Are you sure?" I asked, as the small flame in Hector's thumb flickered and went out. "Look at the size of those hands! Surely it would take little effort for Hector to pummel a man to death."

"At times I wonder, Danvers, whether you ever listen to me at all. Hector is no more capable of pummeling a man than an armoire would be. I ask you: have we seen any movements that resemble martial blows from this automaton?" I had to admit that we had not.

We turned to the second automaton, the one with the more human form and bronze plating, as well as what I would call a design more suited to elicit a proper distinction of class. In his smooth and bowed shape there was an aspect of servitude that I found soothing. Wright switched it on. Its eyes lit up with a yellow glow and as its first action it gave a small bow.

"State your name, automaton."

"Bellamy, sir." Its voice was mechanical yet somehow studied, as if it learned proper intonation from an elocution coach.

"Bellamy. What is your function?"

"I am designated a gentleman's gentleman, sir. Duties include but are not limited to dressing, attending, feeding, and protecting my master from the rigors of the road and the unpleasantness of everyday life."

"Protecting?"

"Yes sir."

"Give examples."

"If it should begin to rain …" and at this Bellamy lifted its left hand, and with an elegant whirl an umbrella extended upwards from its wrist. It unfurled, then with another click the automaton shut and retracted it. "If sir should complain of ennui," and with that Bellamy began to sing, in a surprisingly rich tenor, the music hall favorite "She Was Only a Clacker's Daughter," until with some irritation Wright interrupted.

"Enough of that. Bellamy."

"Sir."

"Are you capable of any physical action that as part of your code to protect your master could result in intentional injury to another person?"

Bellamy extended its left hand and produced a small flame.

"Aside from that," said Wright.

With a click and a whir, Bellamy's torso opened, revealing two small shelves filled with metal containers. It reached inside itself with its left hand and produced a bottle which it dexterously unscrewed, while its right hand reached inside and extracted a small metal thermos. It poured for a three count from the bottle into the thermos, then replaced the bottle and produced a smaller flask whose top when unscrewed revealed a small eyedropper. With the same efficiency it added several drops of liquid to the thermos. As soon as it replaced the small bottle it grasped the thermos in both hands and gave it a ferocious shaking for several seconds. When finished, it poured the clear liquid into a small steel cup and passed it to Wright.

He sniffed it and passed it to me. "Please confirm my suspicions, Danvers. As you know my senses of smell and taste can both be eccentric."

I sniffed. "Vodka, I believe."

"With three drops of Vermouth," said Bellamy. "I have been informed that more than two drinks of this potency can cause damage to a human being, yet I have also been told to provide any guest of Master's choosing as many of these as he requests and I have in stock."

"Therefore resulting in injury to another human being," said Wright.

"Sir is correct."

"Half a moment," I interjected. "Bellamy, what actions would you be allowed to take in defense of yourself?"

"I have been instructed to avoid damage to myself where and when possible, unless it is sustained by the actions of a human being."

"So if you were ordered to leap off a vast cliff by a human being, would you?"

There was a moment while Bellamy performed internal calculations, and then he answered. "I would attempt to make it known to sir that his instruction was liable to be hazardous to my continuance as a functioning automaton, but assuming he was unmoved or simply repeated his command, I would perform the action."

"So you would not and could not defend yourself from damage knowingly delivered onto you by your Master or another human being," asked Wright.

"And what if your Master is beset by physical violence?" I asked. At this the machine began to emit a loud high-pitched klaxon. I waved my hands, and it stopped.

"Again, it seems unlikely that Bellamy could be our culprit, unless as an accessory to the crime of serving the professor an excess of spirits," said Wright. "Yet to be sure ..." and with that, Wright swung his walking stick with the whole force of his mechanical arm behind it at Bellamy's right side. It collided with enough force to topple the unfortunate machine to the ground, where it lay, its plating slightly bent from the impact.

After a moment it spoke, unmoving, from the floor. "Would sir require anything else?"

Assured that Bellamy was incapable of any offensive actions even in defense of himself, we now approached the third automaton, which Wright activated with a flick of its switch, located behind its left ear. Her face—for I could not fail to think of it as feminine—featured an exquisite amount of decorative detail, as if she were a porcelain doll re-imagined in copper and bronze. After a moment a faint whine indicated the mechanism's engine had engaged, light came to its green eyes and it blinked, tiny metal shutters rolling briefly down then up in an uncannily realistic fashion.

"Automaton, state your name and purpose."

"I am Monique, Sir."

Both Wright and I gave a start. The machine's voice was unexpectedly modulated and warm, with an indisputably feminine quality. If a machine could be said to speak with a wiggle, this one did.

"And your purpose?"

"To serve as a maid for a gentleman's household."

"Detail to us your duties."

Monique then inventoried her duties and tasks, from preparing a water basin to emptying chamber pots, from airing laundry to polishing silverware. It was a lengthy list and I'll confess that to hear it all in such explicit detail made me grateful that I have never been forced by circumstance or fortune into domestic servitude.

When she completed her list, Wright asked, "And is this a complete list of your duties?"

"As a maid, yes sir."

"Does this mean that you have duties outside of serving as a maid?"

"Yes sir."

"And what are they?"

"To act as a gentleman's companion."

"What do you mean?"

"For the relief of my Master's tension and cares after a day's work."

Both of us looked at each other. "Detail what tasks this might require," said

Wright. She began to do so.

I had heard of automatons being enlisted into unseemly activities, but assumed that such stories were nothing more than the ribald apocrypha of my club's smoking room. To hear that machine explain just how she would address the needs of an amorous owner was a disturbing education in a particular strain of depravity, a knowledge I would happily forget.

Yet there was nothing in this obscene catalogue dictated by the automaton's code that could have resulted in the brutal injuries suffered by Professor Quire. When she finished, Wright turned the automaton off, with a small nod of reflexive courtesy. "While it cannot be said that Monique is incapable of actions that would be hazardous to a man, they would not involve external bludgeoning. Therefore, I must assume she is not our murderer."

"But look here, Wright, it's got to be one of them. Or, I don't know, all three?"

"Impossible. What's more, I examined the hands of each. Though we were told that the injuries were bloody, none of the automatons have so much as a speck of blood or other tell-tale matter on them."

"But the Inspector explicitly told us that there was no other way in or out of the room."

"All the more reason, then, to move quickly on to the scene of the murder. With any luck his men have left a stray clue untrod by their blundering."

I followed Wright down the corridor to the Inspector's office. We entered to find him sitting at his desk alone, with no sign of the Brigadier. "And where is our military advisor?" asked Wright.

"Returned to file a report. What are the results of your interrogations, Wright?"

"I find no evidence that any of the three automatons that you brought in for inspection were capable of the murder," he said.

"Not capable? Surely any of the three are physically capable of battering the poor man to death."

"In theory, yes. But none of them has as part of their integral code the ability to cause such damage to a human being. Incidentally, there is no physical evidence on the hands of any of them, which confirms that none of the three is our guilty party."

"I am afraid I disagree," said a figure at the door, a muscular young man wearing a cleric's collar. "The use of aether to power automatons is both a physical and moral hazard, and it is no surprise that one of these creations has turned upon its master. You are Ponder Wright, I believe. I have heard of you."

"And judging by your dress and your presence in a police station, you are Prester

Johnson, also known as 'The Spiritualist Detective.'"

"My reputation precedes me," said Johnson, inclining his head, "and your ... unique appearance yours. Happy to meet you." He approached and shook hands with both Wright and myself, then turned to Garrison. "Inspector, I am ready to examine the crime scene."

Wright smiled. "I am as well, Inspector. We are done here."

Garrison shook his head. "Not necessary for you to inspect the site, Wright. As I've said, the room was a hermetically sealed chamber, and the placement of the body rules out accident," he said. "If you can't discover which of the automata is the culprit, we must find other detectives who can."

"Then what is the esteemed Mr. Johnson's reason for examining the scene?"

Johnson gave us both a friendly smile. "For me to practice my calling, I must have access to the greatest possible focus of spiritual energy. In this case, the room in which poor Professor Quire left material existence clearly promises the best results."

"Ah," said Wright, nodding. "Well, that is a refreshingly rational argument, particularly from a man of the Spiritualist persuasion. Perhaps you'll allow me to accompany you on your investigation?"

Johnson understood a challenge had been made. "I will allow it, though the presence of non-believers is not advisable during my work. However, if you are willing to be unobtrusive and refrain from all thoughts of a negative nature during my seanceic duties, you are welcome to accompany me."

"I will be as quiet and unobtrusive as a mechanical mouse," said Wright.

The agreement made, we returned to our cab and instructed it to take us to Professor Quire's house while Johnson and the Inspector travelled by separate coach.

Wright smiled as we sat down across from each other. "I certainly never thought I'd be sitting in on a séance as part of my work in detection," he shouted to me over the engine. "Lord save us. A Spiritualist Detective!"

"Well, there's got to be something in it," I yelled back. "What about ectoplasm? Your own mechanical parts wouldn't work without its presence in your aetheric batteries. And we wouldn't know about it at all if it weren't for the work of Spiritualists."

"Nonsense," shouted Wright. "It is simply a quirk that the celebrated Professor Lodge, whose experiments with electricity led to his discovery of what he called 'ectoplasm,' is a Spiritualist. We understand its value as a source for powering certain machinery, but we know practically nothing of the so-called "Aethereal Plane" from which ectoplasm is harvested. Certainly we have no evidence that the spirits of the departed know anything of it either. Ectoplasm is bound by the same natural laws that govern all things. We are scientists, Danvers, and the answers to any questions of the material world, including murder, are inevitably mundane. Ghosts need not apply."

We were met at the door of the murdered man's home by Garrison, Johnson and the aged housekeeper Mrs. Tilton. Though she stared with trepidation at Wright, in truth she was a much more unsettling sight, with her gray hair a disarrayed mass half in and half sprouting from her cap. We entered the aged townhouse and I realized that its interior luminescence was not from gas lamps, but from large glass globes fixed at regular intervals along the hallway.

"Electrical lighting, I see," said Wright. "I was not aware that this neighborhood was supplied with a power plant."

"It isn't," said the Inspector. "The Professor has his own generator in a back room. Isn't that right, Mrs. Tilton?" The housekeeper nodded vigorously.

"It runs on some sort of fluid that the Professor has brought in," she said. "Black as pitch and smells worse. When I came in this morning, the machine had run down and I had to refill it. Thank goodness I know the house well enough that I could find my way back to the oil lamps in the dark."

"Was it usual for the generator to run out of its fuel?" asked Wright.

"No sir," she said. "The professor was regular as clockwork in making sure that it was filled each night before he went to bed. Though it had been having problems as of late. Once or twice when I was in the house it would go all dark for a minute or two. Then the professor would give a curse and scurry to the machine, give it a bit of a fiddle, and it would start right up again." She indicated a small tin box in her hand. "It's why I never walk about the house without me matchbox in me apron."

"And how long does it take for the generator to burn through its fuel?"

"Three days, as a rule. That's what I recall him saying. When I went down this morning the tank was empty, so I believe he must have last filled it on Thursday night."

Garrison nodded. "And that puts the time of death as around forty-eight to seventy-two hours ago, which corroborates what Mickey back at the morgue said."

"It is fortunate that it was not any longer," said Johnson. "Three days is nearing the lifespan of a psychic echo."

"I did not realize that the science of the Spiritualist movement was so precise on such matters," said Wright.

Johnson nodded solemnly. "As with so many other matters in our Church, seanceic practices are the result of rigorous experimentation. Now, please lead us to the place where the professor left his earthly vessel."

The housekeeper led us through the luxurious if somewhat sterile parlor down a short corridor to the basement door. The hinges on the outside of the door had been removed, and the Inspector pulled it open from this side. "Key, still in the lock," he said, indicating, "just as we found it." He reached inside the door frame and threw a switch, turning on the electrical lights.

Before us was a small landing, from which descended a set of slatted wooden stairs, flanked on each side by a heavy wooden banister that ran all the way down to the floor on each side. The Inspector pointed at the floor of the landing, where a sizable stain of dried blood was still visible. "That's where the body was found, crumpled. You can see the bloodstain on the top stair there, which seeped into the wood. There's another one about halfway down the stairwell where we think the initial attack must have occurred. Lying next to him was this," he said, producing a small pewter candleholder—notably dented—and half a candle.

"Next to him, you say?" asked Wright.

"Well, one step down from him, but yes."

"Please, Inspector, I must ask you to always be as specific as you can," said Wright with some irritation. "If I am not allowed to examine a crime scene as soon as possible after it is discovered, I would at least ask that the details of the scene be accurate." With that he reached up to his right cheek and dialed his magnification lens into place, then began walking down the stairs, scanning as he went.

As he left, Johnson set down his black Gladstone and opened it, bringing out a collection of white candles, which he set in a circle around the bloodstain. He then drew out a small incense brazier, and began to fill it with a collection of dried twigs and herbs. Having briefly had a career as an Anglican altar boy in my village church, I was interested to see what rituals the Spiritualists had adopted from more familiar branches of Christianity, yet as he continued his preparations he glanced up at me with the air of a conjuror seeking some privacy as he assembles his entertainment. I gave an embarrassed smile and started down the stairs after my friend.

Wright was making slow progress, scanning the steps as he went, and was only now approaching the bottom of the stairs. "Go ahead, and I'll catch up," he muttered as I came up to him, so I continued down into the mechanist's laboratory, a looming chamber dominated by four large tables on which were lain a bewildering collection of machinery. I have no doubt that Professor Quire must have had either an astonishing memory or an equally astounding personal filing system, for I confess I could make no sense out of the piles of gears, sprockets, springs, flywheels, crankshafts and far less recognizable items that lay piled on every surface.

I was examining some of these when Wright joined me, then motioned to a blank space at the back wall flanked by an assortment of partial automaton bodies. "That is where the three automatons we examined once stood," he said, and walked back to them, with me following. When he reached the space he turned and looked from this position to the stairway. "Possible, if not likely, Danvers," he said, pointing at the path we had wended to reach the spot.

"What would be possible?" I asked.

"For the crime to be committed here and the body taken to the stairway."

"But the bloodstains are on the stairs, so that's where he must have been killed."

"You might think so and our Inspector does, but the blood trail on the stairs is more perplexing than illuminating."

"Why perplexing?" I asked.

He shook his head. "They make no sense. Some lead between the two large stains. Others appear almost randomly. What's more, the drips are not regular. They appear elongated and smeared."

"By the murderer's feet?"

"Perhaps. Yet why would the murderer make multiple trips up and down the staircase after killing the professor?"

"We are here to solve a mystery, Wright, not find new ones."

"But every new mystery is a clue to the correct solution, Danvers. Now. Let us determine if this chamber is indeed as hermetically sealed as advertised." He turned his attention to the walls of the room, which he began to slowly pace along, his mechanical eye making a series of whirring noises as he utilized its spectrometer, no doubt seeking where variants in heat might indicate a hidden door.

After several minutes Garrison called from the landing above. "Gentlemen? I believe we are ready." As I ascended the stairs I noticed Wright stopping to look at an ornamental section of the staircase's banister. He seemed intrigued by some particular detail, but as I looked back at him he waved me to continue upwards.

As I ascended I saw that Johnson had changed into a dark cloak with a single white line on its front, which radiated outwards at the middle of the back like a star. He had just concluded lighting the candles he'd set on the floor. He struck a match and set the contents of his censer alight, and as the incense began to billow he swung it out in a circle. As smoke began to fill the landing, through it came Wright, who took up a position next to me, watching Johnson's efforts with an expression of mild interest.

The priest addressed us. "I shall now attempt to find the spirit of the unfortunate man in the Aethereal realm, and return him to our plane of existence so that we may communicate. Be warned that if I am successful, he shall only be present for a minute or two at most. The spirits of the dead do not like to tarry on this plane once they have glimpsed Summerland."

With the scented smoke now thick about us he began a sort of low chanting. Having little facility with Latin in school I had no idea what the words were. But the effect was indeed eerie, whatever was being said. Johnson's eyes glazed, and his entire visage seemed to slowly empty itself out of personality as he droned on. Then I shivered with the fear of the uncanny, for there seemed now to be another face behind the face of the priest, animating it. When he spoke, it was with an old man's voice, quavering and unsure, with the very cadence altered completely from Johnson's own.

"Who ... where ... Ah. You have called, and I answer. Why have you pulled my weary spirit back from the path to bliss?"

Garrison, ever the professional, spoke in a steady tone, though I could tell he found the moment as eerie and as unsettling as I. "Professor. We seek your murderer. Can you tell us what you saw and felt in the moments prior to your death?"

The priest looked about, his eyes blank and unseeing. "Then I am dead. I had forgotten. It is ... painful to remember. And to be back here."

"Please, sir," continued Garrison, "we wish to bring the culprit to justice. Tell us who did this to you."

Johnson's face, which had turned sorrowful, now began to shake. "Not a who. An it. No living being ended my life. But my creation, my beautiful creation. ..."

"One of the automatons, then? Which one? Which of the three?"

Johnson's face continued to shake with increasing violence, and he spoke between spasmodic shudders. "It was ... it was ... as I ascended. From behind the sound, then I stumbled, then the crash on my head ... oh God, murdered by my own ... I am dead? Too painful, no, too painful. I cannot. I cannot stay!" and with a cry the priest's head jerked up, then dropped back into his chest. He opened his eyes and looked at us, sweating and blinking.

"Was he here? Did he speak?"

"He did indeed, Father," said Garrison. "And he confirmed it was one of the automatons."

"An impressive display," said Wright, "if I was a man of a sufficiently open mind. But alas as you have surmised, Mr. Johnson, I am an inevitable cynic about this and so many other things."

"You accuse me of being a charlatan?" asked Johnson, in a surprisingly even tone.

"No," said Wright. "For all I know you entirely believe in your own powers, which to my definition a charlatan would not. But there was nothing in what you said that gave any evidence of knowledge garnered from the deceased professor."

"Then you believe that the spirit I summoned did not speak the truth?"

Wright held up his human hand. "I did not say that. In fact I have reason to believe that what you said while in your trance was very possibly the truth, as vague as it was."

"So you think one of the Professor's automatons was indeed the murderer?" asked Garrison. "But I thought you said that they're innocent."

"Oh, none of them are in any way guilty," said Wright, "though it is ridiculous to speak about such human attributes as 'innocence' or 'guilt' when speaking of an automaton. No, I believe that I have found the murderer, and it is indeed one of the Professor's own creations."

"Explain yourself, Wright," said Garrison.

"All right then," he said, leaning against the banister behind him. "We have been told that the Professor's corpse revealed the effects of a severe beating, of blows administered to a variety of regions of his body, in particular a fatal strike to the back of his head. This is undoubtedly what killed him, but it was no automaton that delivered the blows." He gestured behind him to the stairway. "Inspector, you noted a bloodstain under the body on the landing and another significant stain halfway down the staircase, correct?"

Garrison looked down the stairs. "I did. That was the evidence that the Professor was initially struck from behind as he ascended the stairway. The body fell, then after it received additional blows from the murderer, it was lifted and carried up to the landing."

Wright smiled. "Yet how does that make sense? You have not suggested that the Professor was deaf or hard-of-hearing. If he was attacked as he climbed the stairs, surely he would have heard the sound of one of his automatons as it followed behind him, yes?"

"Perhaps he programmed it to follow him, and the traitorous machine struck him when he least expected," said Johnson.

"An admirable conjecture, and I suppose that might be possible," agreed Wright, "if one were to ignore the additional drops of blood that I found below that middle stain. Or the fact that these stains were all elongated, as if they had run not down a stairway but down a flat surface."

"What? That makes no sense," said Garrison.

Wright nodded. "Indeed, given the scenario you outlined, it makes no sense whatsoever. Yet if you examine the stairs carefully you'll see that I am correct. And this led me to the discovery of the murderer."

"What are you saying, Wright?" said Johnson.

My friend turned again to Garrison. "Let me ask you a riddle. What's the difference between a set of stairs going down and a set of stairs going up?"

Garrison frowned and considered. "It's all about which direction you're taking them, I suppose."

"With ordinary stairs I would agree with you, Inspector." And with that he began descending the steps. When he reached the bottom he called up to us, "Yet these are not ordinary stairs." I started to descend but he held up his hand. "All of you stand on the landing, if you please. I have something to demonstrate."

He began to fiddle with the ornamentation of the banister. After a moment there was a creak, then a monstrous groan, and then to our astonishment the stairs began to move ... towards us!

"Meet the murderer of the unfortunate Professor," yelled Wright from below. "One of his most brilliant inventions, a mechanical moving staircase. A continuous chain of steps, powered by a hidden motor, which rise, or descend, into the floor, depending on the direction they are set. No doubt a commission from Harrods or another of Quire's commercial contracts. Such a device designed to efficiently move customers with minimum physical exertion will no doubt prove highly popular when it makes its eventual appearance in the halls of commerce."

He stepped onto the moving staircase and was carried up to us at walking speed.

"But how was it activated?" asked Garrison as Wright reached us on the landing, stepping back onto the unmoving surface with élan.

"That I cannot say. My assumption is that due to one of his generator's recent failings, power to the engine was shut off, perhaps in mid-operation. The Professor, left alone in the dark of his laboratory, lit a candle and started up the now static staircase to make his way to the generator. But when he was halfway up, the generator began again, and with a lurch the stairs began to move. He fell backwards, hit his head, and then his body continued to be buffeted by a series of blows. In effect he fell down this single stairway dozens, perhaps hundreds, of times."

"Remarkable!" said Garrison, his eyes still fixed on the Professor's inadvertently deadly invention.

"Indeed," said Wright. "Inspector, you may tell the Brigadier that Quince was successful not only in his commission for the Army, but in creating a machine that could kill. I would however add that it's not one they'll have much luck testing on the battlefield."

Back at our sitting room on Clacker Street, Wright and I sat musing next to the fire, each supplied with a whiskey and soda. As was his custom he added both lime and bitters to his—something about the metals used to reconstruct his face affected his palate in unique ways.

"A classic case of technophobia, my dear Danvers. Ever since the days of the unfortunate Dr. Victor Frankenstein the populace has had a fear of our mechanical creations turning on us."

"And don't you, Wright? After all, you are intimately aware of how effective our machinery is in performing any human task. It is inevitable that we shall make automatons that can kill, isn't it?"

"Inevitable, yes. From the scythe to the blasting cap we have a genius for making our tools lethal. Yet no one has ever been able to replicate Frankenstein's experiments, and for all we know the story of his monster may be either fraud or a gross exaggeration. I don't myself believe we'll ever see a machine capable of the conscious malice and cruelty of Man."

"No," I agreed. "Nor his perversity. When I think of the Professor's work, the one that disturbs me the most is Monique."

"Me as well, my friend. Let us be thankful, then, that unlike automatons, we are capable of the great and terrible responsibility of free will."

"One final question, Wright. I noticed before we left that you took Johnson aside for a quick chat. What was that about?"

My friend smiled. "A short financial discussion, nothing more. I was interested in learning what rates the good priest was routinely receiving from the Yard for his consultations."

"Oh? To what purpose?"

"It is important in a buyer's market to know both one's own worth and the value of one's competition. And when I told Johnson I would be happy to make a contribution equal to whatever the difference might be to his Church, he readily agreed."

"So even a man of the cloth is amenable to financial persuasion," I said.

"Oh, he's not a bad sort," said Wright. "What's more, nothing he said, through conscious or unconscious means, actually contradicted the solution. Perhaps I was too hasty in condemning him and his craft. At the very least, he was able to persuade the constabulary to receive access to a crime scene. Perhaps I shall add 'mechanical divination' to my list of proffered services."

As he spoke, the gasogene in the corner gave a small hiss through its nozzle. "You see? He agrees with me," he said. "And what's more, he's asking if you can add a bit more whiskey to my glass." Though I knew he jested, I gave the contraption a wide berth as I crossed to the liquor cabinet.

WHO MADE SHERLOCK'S CLAY PIPE?

Bruce Harris

There are questions and there are burning questions. "I always smoke 'ship's' myself," states Dr. John H. Watson in the first Sherlock Holmes adventure, *A Study in Scarlet*. Good to know, but hardly a question, yet researchers pursued. To what did Watson refer when he said, 'ship's'? Tobacco? A pipe? Not to mention his usage of the Delphic three apostrophes in a five-letter word?

Two phrases, the ubiquitous "Elementary, My Dear Watson," and the rara avis, "I Always Smoke Pollack's myself," never crossed Sherlock Holmes's lips. But, the latter could (and should) have been the detective's response to his chronicler's 'ship's' confession during their first historic meeting.

Sherlock Holmes reached for his clay pipe more than any other type of pipe, yet little effort has been made to identify the maker of the "old and oily clay pipe." Holmes's clay is mentioned in six cases. While attempts have been made to identify Holmes's briar wood pipes, the same attention has not been afforded the "old black (clay) pipe." Outside the Sherlockian world, a plethora of information and research are available for clay pipes versus all other pipe types. Perhaps too much information exists causing researchers to shy away? With the ever-present renewed interest in Sherlock Holmes, the brand of the detective's clay is a burning question not being addressed by literature-loving devotees worldwide.

During the 19th century, clay was by far the most common material from which pipes were made. More than 535 makers of clay pipes existed in the city of London alone between the years 1800–1899! It is possible to trace as many as 3,400 clay pipe makers in England during this period. A singular group they were. Included among their number were a murderer (Thomas Morgan), a thief (Daniel Smith), and an escaped felon (Richard Owen). How does one go about narrowing down such an enormous and eclectic field? Let's key on one of these pipe makers, Pollock.

There are facts suggesting that the Pollock factory produced Holmes's clay pipes. More accurately, Edward Pollock of the Central Clay Pipe Works (the name was changed to John Pollock in 1928) of Manchester is the likely source for Holmes's clays. Edward Pollock began producing pipes in 1879, about the same time Holmes was beginning his detective career and the same time a certain Professor James Moriarty (one of two Moriarty brothers named James) arrived in London. Pollock pipes were heavily marketed and advertised. Not only would Holmes have been familiar with Pollock's advertising, he would have been drawn to Pollock for another, surreal reason. Edward Pollock's first three children were all named James! Surely, this is something Holmes would find sufficiently quirky and could not, would not, ignore. Until contrary evidence is presented, let's assume Holmes reached for his Pollock whenever he reached for a clay pipe.

Clay pipes were often described as black, but the black clay may not be merely discolored pre-smoked white clay. Rather, clay pipes were originally made black in color at the factory. Clays were also produced in a variety of colors, including white, red, brown, and black. These colored pipes helped alleviate the monotony of producing the same standard white clays while at the same time satisfying the needs and wants of the pipe smoking public. Pollock's Central Clay Pipe Works produced such colored pipes, including black.

Holmes's oily clay may have come from a faulty mould in Pollock's factory. Moulds were made to specifications. Four parts paraffin oil (Coleman's white kerosene) and one part rapeseed oil was used in the clay moulds during the 1800s. The overly oily pipe owned by Holmes may have been formed from a mould smeared with an incorrect ratio of oil types and subjected to a lapse in quality control during production.

"The Adventure of the Red-Headed League" is the source of the famous Sherlock Holmes, "three-pipe problem." Explanation? Two possibilities exist. First, Holmes smoked three bowls in fifty minutes. Unlikely. That calculates to less than 17 minutes per bowl. In other words, Holmes smoked small-bowled pipes. A second and more plausible explanation is that Holmes smoked a clay pipe with three bowls! "Multiple bowled [clay] pipes were made in late 19th century England ... among them is a three-bowled specimen," writes Richard Le Cheminant in a 1985 article for the *Society for Clay Pipe Research*.

A vivid image of Holmes with his clay pipe appears in "The Adventure of the Red-Headed League" with the words, "... [the clay pipe was] thrusting out like the bill of some strange bird." One school of thought, originating here, is that Holmes is actually smoking a carved bird's head pipe. Such a pipe is not fantasy. Paul S. Jung, Jr. in his 2003, *Pollock's of Manchester: Three Generations of Clay Tobacco Pipemakers*. Archaeopress, points out that Samuel McLardy, who set up shop in Manchester in 1865, produced clay pipes in the shape of a fowl's head. Although competitors, Pollock and McLardy often cooperated with each other, sharing supplies and producing special orders to satisfy each other's customers. Perhaps it is a carved fowl head pipe, complete with beak, described by Watson in "The Adventure of the Red-Headed League?"

Despite the profusion of studies involving Sherlock Holmes and smoking, very little research about the makers of the great detective's clay pipes exist. With one or two exceptions, no attempt has been made to classify Holmes's clay pipes, until now.

John Hall's 1994 tome, *140 Different Varieties—A Review of Tobacco in the Canon*, articulates a challenge. "... Modest Sherlockian fame awaits any scholar who can crack the A.D.P. acronym of [John] Straker's briar." Straker is a character in the Sherlock Holmes adventure, "Silver Blaze." Had Straker's pipe been made of clay, the enigmatic *Archer Donovan Pipe* would be the likely answer of the A.D.P. mystery. A not uncommon clay pipe depicts jockey Fred Archer and racehorse Donovan. Winner of the Derby and St. Leger in 1889, Donovan was born in the spring of 1886. Celebrated jockey Fred Archer committed suicide at age 29 in November 1886. Archer never rode Donovan, yet the two appear on the same pipe bowl. Is it coincidence that "Silver Blaze" is a racehorse? Alas, time will tell what awaits the scholar who cracks the identity of Holmes's clay pipe.

LONDON AFTER MIDNIGHT

Ralph E. Vaughan

Contrary to popular thought, Dr John H Watson was not Sherlock Holmes's only friend in London, nor his sole narrator. There were times when Watson, whose outlook was as pragmatic as Holmes's, would have been baffled by events, as in the incident at the Natural History Museum. There, Holmes turned to Roger Sherrington, a clubman of some note, a gentleman of independent means, and a scholar of ancient books, arcane mythologies, and vanished civilizations. He was the polar opposite of Holmes, a whimsical arch-romantic and a believer in many odd, occult and bizarre notions. He had an intuitive understanding of the world that ran counter to Holmes's analytical mind, and while we might at times consider him a flippant and 'unreliable narrator,' he provided, for some of the events that night, a point of view of which Sherlock Holmes himself was quite incapable of achieving.

Sherlock Holmes believes me a fool. Once, he actually voiced that opinion, though not in an entirely unkind tone, and at the time I could hardly contest the charge. Be that as it may, I felt he at least understood my sincerity even if he did not give any credence to my admittedly odd beliefs. I knew he would never budge from his Gibraltar of Logic, that unassailable redoubt of rationality from which he surveys and judges the world, just as I would never abandon my belief in a cadre of banished monster-gods awaiting the proper alignment of stars to reestablish their rule over Earth for the purpose of enslaving and devouring humanity.

Ah, yes, admittedly odd.

I well know how such outré ideas might rest with even the most liberal-minded, but I never would have accused Holmes of having such a mind. His was the keenest intellect of his age, and I always counted humanity fortunate his nature dictated a predilection toward law and order rather than crime and world domination. Me, I would have been constantly tempted. I assumed Sherlock Holmes and I would forever be at antipodes of belief and philosophy.

As it turned out, I was mistaken.

At least I think so, though, even now, I cannot say with any great confidence what beliefs truly reside in that magnificent mind of his. In any age, Sherlock Holmes will ever be the Great Enigma.

It was late one autumn night, 1898, as I prepared to retire. An urgent knocking sounded at my Westminster Mansions flat. I waved off my man, Giles, who himself was making to retire for the night, and answered it.

"Good, you're at home, Sherrington," Sherlock Holmes said to me. "Grab your hat and coat, we must hurry!"

"But where, Holmes?" I cried, even as I scurried to collect my outer garments. "What has happened?"

"A death," he explained.

"A murder?" I jammed on my hat and struggled into my coat.

"Perhaps," he replied cryptically. "Hurry, man!"

"Well, can you at least tell me where we are going?"

"The Natural History Museum, South Kensington."

We bustled out the door. "Who was killed? How? Why?"

"There is no time for explanations."

Just as I was about to close the door, a hand shot out bearing my Webley-Fosbery Automatic. I stuffed it into my coat pocket.

"Very good idea, Giles," I murmured.

"Yes, I thought so, sir," my man replied in that dry, even tone he used for announcing brunches and the end of the world.

The door closed, the latch shot, and I hurried to catch Holmes, who had already clattered down to the first floor. I finally caught up with him at ground level, nearly out of breath—me not him—and followed him into an evil night of yellowish roiling fog.

A hansom waited. At Holmes's approach, the driver at the rear of the fly vehicle pulled a lever, opening the low panels at the front. I followed him in immediately, but so quickly did the cabby push the lever back into place I was nearly snapped in a most indelicate fashion, if you know what I mean.

"Natural History Museum," Holmes called up through the trap. "Exhibition Road, near the Southern Galleries, via the Imperial Institute Road."

The trap shut like a crack of thunder and we were off.

"Holmes, surely the Museum's frontage is on Cromwell Road."

"We shan't use that entrance for reasons which will become obvious," Holmes explained, explaining nothing, as usual.

"Really, Holmes, this is most irregular," I chided. "I don't mind being dragged into this pea-soup particular at less than a moment's notice, even though you've deprived me of chugging my nightly g-and-t, but at least you can explain why you have picked on *me*, of all people. Watson have influenza or beriberi or some such rot?"

Holmes uttered a sharp laugh. As usual, it was difficult to tell whether I had amused him or if he was merely clearing his sinuses.

"No, Watson is quite hale and hearty, currently at home with wife number six ..." He stroked his chin. "Well, she is not quite a proper replacement, so let us be charitable and call her wife number five-and-a-half. No matter. This night I need neither physician nor biographer, but a man knowledgeable about the Noctis Shards."

"Really, Holmes!" I snapped peevishly. "I know you believe me a rather gullible specimen of humanity, but I see no reason to mock me!"

"Not at all, my dear fellow," Holmes assured me.

"Holmes, there are two things I know as absolute facts," I said. "You do not trouble yourself about any academic discipline that does not aid you in apprehending evil-doers, and ..."

"That is not quite ..." he started to protest.

I whipped toward him, as much as was possible in the confines of the hansom, and demanded: "What celestial body rests at the center of our solar system?"

"The sun," he replied after a moment, a moment too long to my way of thinking.

"Learned that to embarrass Watson, did you?" I accused. "Well, never mind. You are completely disinterested in anything supernatural, so why trouble yourself about the Noctis Shards? Mentioned by the Romans, but not discovered until the French occupation of Egypt, they tell how the Great Old Ones came to the Old Kingdom, Fifth Dynasty to be specific, and how Pharaoh Neferirkare defeated them in 2471 BC, driving them into the Outer Darkness."

"Surely, the right man for the job," Holmes said. "Since the Noctis Shards address mythological and supernatural issues, they are without practical value. Obviously, you did not let that stop *you* from studying them."

"True," I agreed, ignoring his left-handed compliment. "Having studied them, I know the Shards were lost in 1803, when LaSalle went mad and slaughtered his expedition. I know they were never properly translated and now exist as drawings—obverses only, not reverses, present whereabouts unknown."

"You are correct in every respect," he replied dryly, "but one."

"And which is that?" I tried to match his tone, and failed.

"In believing the Noctis Shards lost."

"What?"

"They are currently in the possession of Sir Charles Leigh, the Museum's General Librarian," Holmes said.

I was at a loss for words. Well, not entirely, and not for long, for after I closed my gaping mouth I said: "I should have brought some of my files, but, no matter, I can get those later. This is quite the opportunity of a lifetime."

"Actually, we have not the luxury of a lifetime, my dear chap," Holmes said. "Should we fail to resolve this mystery by midnight, there might be more deaths." He hesitated. "And such terror as your imagination could not possibly conceive."

Actually, I have a vivid imagination. Envisioning the horrors of an impersonal, often-hostile cosmos is rather a forte of mine, but I held silent, not wanting to intrude upon Holmes's discomfort or my own moment. The Noctis Shards! Access to such a trove of arcane lore was the fondest desire, or certainly one of them, of every occultist and scholar, though I rather considered myself to be more the latter than the former, if you know what I mean.

As the hansom clattered around a corner, Holmes elbowed me and directed my attention into the night. The fog had mostly lifted during our journey, but it was still like peering through a veil. I recognized the bulk of the Natural History Museum, though I could see only part of its seven-hundred foot frontage, nor the entirety of the two-hundred-foot towers, but what I could view of the façade was decidedly odd ... quite deucedly odd!

"Holmes, it appears the entrance is blocked by scaffolding of some sort," I ventured. "Is that the reason ..."

"Look more closely, Sherrington," Holmes advised. "Despite the obscurity you should be able to observe, and deduce."

I returned my attention to the façade, eager to see what Holmes saw before the hansom bore us away. There was no moon, of course, and the museum was shrouded in gloom, but there was a faint wash of gaslight from along the roadway. No, not scaffolding, as I had first thought. The forms lacked angularity and rigidity. Ropes? I dismissed the idea as quickly as it popped into my mind as monkeys make totally unsuitable workmen. I observed a regularity and complexity that suggested the application of sound engineering principles. If anything, they looked very much like ...

The front of the museum passed out of sight as I sputtered and tried to give voice to my notion. The very ludicrousness of the result lodged in my mind, preventing me from speaking. I looked back to Holmes, eyes wide with excitement. I was not at all amused to see the faint suggestion of a smile upon Holmes's lips.

"Really, my dear fellow, this is too much!" I snapped. "I would not expect such tomfoolery from you!"

If he was the least bit upset by my outburst he gave no sign. In fact, his eyes twinkled. I often suspected his staid and sober façade hid quite a cheeky monkey tossing coconuts at us mere humans. It certainly explained Holmes's infuriating penchant for asking what a chap had seen, solely for the purpose of telling him what he should have observed. Made me feel sorry for Watson. Almost.

"Very well," I shot into the silence. "It appears as if part of the entrance is covered with … stringy strands."

His eyebrows shot up enquiringly.

"Blast it!" I snapped. "Webs! As if from a ruddy spider!"

The suggestion of a smile hovering about his lips did not actually materialize, but it came very close.

"Go on," I told him. "Shoot me in the heart! Go ahead and tell me what I missed, what I should have observed."

"Well done, Sherrington," he murmured.

My jaw dropped and I protested: "But that's impossible!"

"Any postulation supported by keen observation and deduced by logical extrapolation will never be entirely impossible," Holmes pointed out. "Merely improbable."

"Really, Holmes—a giant spider?"

"Often *highly* improbable," Holmes conceded.

To tell the truth, I found Holmes's apparent approval of my suggestion much more disquieting than any gibe he might toss my way, or even a giant spider for that matter. In my avocation, gibes and scoffs are common, so any sort of encouraging nod, especially from one so grounded in the mundane world as was Sherlock Holmes, was certainly cause for worry.

I was also concerned because the Noctis Shards, fragmentary as they were, contained disturbing hints of an arachnid known by the barbaric name Atlach-Nacha. As I had told Holmes, the Shards had not been translated properly before they vanished during that distasteful incident with Professor LaSalle. As far as the drawings went, they were of disappointing quality and only showed the obverses. Most scholars dismissed them as a hoax perpetrated by LaSalle himself, not entirely unbelievable since he *did* turn out to be a homicidal madman, which is certain to colour one's view of him, if you know what I mean. And he *was* French. Of the occultists who busied themselves with those scribbled drawings, most were more than a little wonky in the bean, even by my own broad and charitable standards. *If* indeed the Shards were once more available for study—not that Mr Sherlock Holmes was ever wrong about anything, not counting of course that embarrassing incident in Norbury—then their long-hidden reverses would be revealed. I could finally solve the mystery of what really happened during the Old Kingdom's Fifth Dynasty, could understand the nature of Atlach-Nacha, and uncover ancient and arcane secrets long hidden from modern man. And, of course, prevent more deaths and forestall such terror as my imagination could not possibly conceive. Yes, we mustn't forget that, must we?

The hansom halted and we clambered out. I looked around. I had been to the museum in the past and once to the Imperial Institute, but I might as well have been dropped in the midst of an alien city. How different everything seems at night, and from an unusual view. So caught up was I in sorting out exactly where I was at the back of the edifice that I did not see a man striding swiftly out of the mist until he was almost upon us.

"Holmes, thank goodness!" the man cried. He was dressed in grey, was stout, slightly under average height, and clean-shaven except for greying muttonchops. Then he started as if seeing me for the first time. "Is this …"

Holmes introduced me to Sir Charles Leigh, director of the general holdings of the museum library.

"So you're the expert on bogies, banshees, and things that go bump in the night," he greeted. "Pleased to meet you."

I looked for some trace of mockery in his demeanor but saw only grim concern. There was a tautness to his jaw, and as he shook my hand I detected a slight tremor. More alarming, though, was a splash of blood upon his cuff, though he appeared uninjured.

"Sir Charles discovered the body," Holmes said.

I realized then that even as I was observing Leigh, Holmes was watching me even more closely. True, I had felt an increasing sense of nervousness and mounting dread, but I was absolutely certain my emotions were under control. Mostly. But I also well realized that when it came to a man like Sherlock Holmes there were few secrets the human heart could hide.

"As you requested, Mr Holmes, I have not notified the police," Leigh reported. "I fear the Board will not …"

"Police tramping about will result in more deaths," Holmes said. "Do not discount the message in blood. Our current measures are sufficient, for now. You agreed to accept my guidance."

"Yes, yes I did." He grabbed his head with both hands, and it seemed to me as if he were about to swoon from the great psychic pressure under which he labored. "Poor Oliphant! Dreadful!"

"Oliphant?" I squeaked. I knew a chap named Oliphant, from my club. He owed me five quid.

"Steady, Leigh," Holmes cautioned in a voice that cut through the man's terror like a scalpel. "You shall be of no use to anyone if you fall to pieces."

"Yes, yes, of course, you are correct, Mr Holmes," Leigh said. He shuddered, but otherwise got a grip on himself, more or less. Stout fellow, stiff upper lip, and all that rot. "It's just that, the state of James's body, the manner in which he was killed …"

James? James Oliphant? Yes, that fiver was most certainly lost.

Holmes in the lead, we headed for the museum's rear entrance.

"Since the way in which he was killed is significant, I want you to see the body first," Holmes said to me. "Then the Noctis Shards."

I gulped nervously. I had no desire to see poor Oliphant brown bread, but Holmes was probably right. He usually was.

"I … I can't take seeing him again, Holmes," Leigh said. He did not look at all well, slightly greenish about the gills, if you know what I mean, very much as I feel when one of my militant aunts issues a summons to visit. "I'll get the Shards for you and …"

"Sherrington," I supplied, trying to eke out a smile and failing miserably. "I'm sure that will be …" I looked to Holmes.

"By all means, Sir Charles," Holmes said.

"In my office then," the old boy murmured, then scarpered.

Holmes ushered me down a staircase into the bowels of the museum. No bally patron ever came down here, I wagered, nor would he want to, what with it all shadowy and cobwebby and lined with crates, some opened like robbed coffins. I walked full face into a web and reacted rather poorly.

"Only a spider's web," Holmes assured me. "A regular spider."

I refrained from telling Holmes what first popped into my mind and instead said: "You're taking this all very calmly, Holmes. I would think a spider even as big as Toby would send you ankling for the nearest exit."

Holmes ignored my gibe, the cad!

"Or maybe you'd just beat it senseless with a singlestick."

Holmes mummied-up and we entered a half-open door. When I saw the corpse on a table I regretted thinking of a gentleman of the pyramids. The body had been wrapped like Tut, but the covering was cut away. His face was sunken and pinched in. Yes, James Oliphant, now beyond all debt collection. Instead of being rolled in linen and stuffed with spices, he was layered with tough silken fibers, now open, revealing wounded chest and bloodied hands.

"I really do hate spiders," I murmured. "Right up there with snakes, millipedes and most of my aunts, but at least Oliphant's fate is in keeping with the Noctis Shards."

"A giant spider?" Holmes asked. "They actually claim that?"

"More or less. The drawings of the Shards are not well done, so it's difficult to tell, but Atlach-Nacha seems to figure in Egypt's Fifth Dynasty brouhaha, back when Neferirkare was the lad with the fake beard."

"Atlach-Nacha is a minion of Cthulhu?"

"You *have* picked up a few things, old bean, likely just to annoy poor Watson, but, yes, a minion of Old Tentacle Chin."

"Cthulhu's cultists would be allied to those of Atlach-Nacha?"

"Yes, if Atlach-Nacha had any," I said. "Not first team. Atlach-Nacha came to Earth from Saturn, then crawled under a mountain in Hyperborea and snoozed. Hardly awe inspiring. Nary a cultist, but with dangerous offspring. If not for what happened in Egypt …"

"Exactly what *did* happen?"

"That is a matter of conjecture," I admitted. "The inscriptions on the Shards—on the *drawings* of the shards, I should say—tell of doorways in space and time, of dark creatures scarpering up and down the Nile, raising a ruckus, avatars of Atlach-Nacha …"

"Not Atlach-Nacha itself?"

"No, mere extensions of the old girl," I said, wishing again I had brought my files. "Like a … oh, I don't know …"

"A spoor of the beast?"

"Odd word, but, yes, I suppose so."

"But Atlach-Nacha *is* a giant spider?" Holmes interrupted, rather a little peevishly, I thought.

"Well, yes, and no," I said. "A spider larger than a carriage, but with a female head. Very dangerous … you know how some chaps will overlook anything for a pretty face. But she's also deadly because of her ability to mesmerize her prey, a form of telepathy."

"And what does the historical record say?"

I grimaced. Why do people always insist upon sources based in reality? "Nothing definite, I fear, just that there was an invasion of dark forces, turned back only by the unconquerable might and irresistible will of Neferirkare, his swift sword and his manly magnificence, et cetera, et cetera, et cetera … I doubt government propaganda will ever change. Most historians dismiss it as a dust-up between Egyptians and some desert barbarians, written up boldly to make the pharaoh seem the golden boy of Ra."

"No spiders in the historical record?"

"Not even an itsy-bitsy one."

"Much less the size of a carriage?"

"No, but even the sage who created the Noctis Shards was a bit conservative about that," I said. "I don't think we're dealing with the original Atlach-Nacha." He gave me a rather questionable look, and I added, quickly: "If the original Atlach-Nacha were here, it would not be hard to find the old girl, toodling through the museum like a pachyderm on parade. No, this is something smaller. I suppose you could call it 'spoor' or some such thing. If I get started on the Shards, perhaps I can be a little more helpful."

Holmes nodded. "Before we join Sir Charles, take a look at what Oliphant wrote."

He conducted me to a space behind some tumbled and shattered crates. There, upon the wall, was bloodily written: *Midnight London Apocalypse Spoor*

"My word, that *is* odd," I remarked, glancing at poor Oliphant. "Must have written it as he was … you know …"

"Oliphant was working in this room when he was attacked," Holmes said. "He retreated behind these crates, wrote this message, then was attacked again. The marks on the wood are identical to the wounds on his chest. He was placed on the table, immobilized with what appears to be webbing, then killed."

"The state of …" I stammered a bit. Though I would never see my five quid again, he had been a decent sort of a chap. And even if he hadn't been, one still had to be loyal to a fellow clubman. "Dash it all, Holmes, why does he look like that?"

"All bodily fluids have been withdrawn."

"Withdrawn?"

"Sucked out."

I felt like ejecting some bodily fluids from my own corpus, but that would have been terribly bad form.

"What do you make of the message, Holmes?"

He frowned. "Oliphant tried to tell us what we faced. He had little time before the second attack. Four words—a deadline, a place, the scope, and something about the nature of our foe."

"Yes, the first three, Holmes, fairly obvious," I agreed, "but what of *Spoor*? What does it mean? I know what appeared in Egypt might have been a kind of spoor, but webbing is also spoor, and that is what he seems wrapped ... Dash it! What was he doing here?"

"Cataloguing artifacts found by the Ferris-Knight Expedition," Holmes replied.

"Knight's a name that's been bandied about on Fleet Street recently, but nothing to do with old Egypt," I said.

"Yes," Holmes agreed. "Professor David Knight died in a fall from his flat in Portman Square."

"Or was he pushed?"

"The flat was locked from within."

"Could he have ..." I made an arching motion with my hand. "Was his swanner a case of self-defenestration?"

"A possibility, but the police think not," Holmes said. "He left no note." As I was about to pose another pointless query, my companion added: "However, a statement from Sir Walter Ferris would reveal the late professor's state of mind."

"He hasn't told anyone?"

"His whereabouts are unknown."

I frowned. "But, wait half-a-mo, Holmes. How do the Shards figure in with that expedition? They were lost decades ago."

"Among the artifacts returned by Ferris and Knight were the Noctis Shards, found in an unopened tomb in Abydos."

"LaSalle was in Egypt when he topped his mates, but in Giza, not Abydos," I protested. "I see how they could have been moved, but how the deuce could they end up in a *sealed* tomb?"

"Sir Charles is baffled, but thinks them authentic," Holmes said. "There is one other thing to show you."

We crossed to a side table covered with pottery and other Old Kingdom flotsam and jetsam. At the end of the table was a sink, clogged with a mixture of stone fragments and a cottony mass.

"What is it?" I asked.

"The fragments comprise a sphere about a foot in diameter, if my calculations are correct, composed of calcium and lime," he said. "As to the other mass ..." He shrugged, which to me was the most unbelievable event of the night. "Chemically, it is identical to the strands around Oliphant and upon the museum exterior, but more supple."

I was boggled by Oliphant's macabre departure from this vale of tears and the idea we might have an eight-legged stalker, but the look on Holmes's face made me think he expected some learned contribution on my part. I felt woefully inadequate.

"Could something have been sealed within the stone sphere?" I suggested. "I can't think how such a trick might be done, but, then, I'm baffled by old salts who put ships in bottles, though I well know how they are emptied in the first place."

"There are no seams on the fragments," Holmes mused. "If two hollowed hemispheres were somehow ..."

"I say, Holmes, do you think we could possibly get on to the Noctis Shards?" I glanced about and nervously touched the Webley-Fosbery in my coat pocket, hoping not to accidentally blow off a finger or some other appendage. "The clock is ticking."

"We've seen all there is to see," Holmes agreed. "Sir Charles thinks the fragments authentic, but I desire your validation."

"Thank you, Holmes, but I might be more helpful if I ..."

"Sir Charles should be able to provide any reference material you need," Holmes said. "This is not the British Museum, but it is well provided with books and manuscripts which would meet with your approval. Be diligent, be accurate, but above all be swift, for as you so aptly said, the clock is ticking."

I was quite happy to be away from poor Oliphant, the remnants of violence, and the last known location of Atlach-Nacha, or at least something very much like it. As we neared the ground level, a thought struck me like the back-kick of a donkey.

"How many people are now in the museum?" I asked.

"Just the three of us," Holmes replied. "I sent away the night staff. All entrances were sealed. The rear door through which we entered is watched over by guards armed with shotguns."

I had not noticed the chaps, but I blamed it on fog, not my confusion and nervousness. We made our way out of the workroom to Sir Charles's office. This time, the way seemed darker, more fraught with moving shadows, disturbed by skittering noises at the edge of silence. More than ever, the crates, opened or not, seemed like waiting coffins. I mentioned none of these impressions to Holmes, however. I refused to give him the satisfaction.

When we entered, Sir Charles stood. "I took the liberty of assembling such reference material as you might need."

The old boy might have been blathering about the weather, the phases of the moon, or a giant spider ready to pounce on me from behind. My attention was focused on the artifacts on the desk, the irregular stone fragments nestled in a low-sided box cushioned with cotton, gleaming beneath two lamps.

"I have not examined them closely myself," he prattled on as I eased him out of my way. "Too disquieting … unsettling …"

I murmured something, probably, "Quite all right, old bean," or something equally silly. To me, the old cod vanished, as did Holmes, the museum, and even the specter of Atlach-Nacha and the prospect of apocalyptic destruction. I confess, my hand trembled as I reached toward the artifacts, something that usually does not occur unless I am invited to the home of one of my aunts (who usually wants me to meet her latest man-hunting heiress friend) or I run out of liquor. Actually, I could have used a bracing b-and-s at the moment, but Sir Charles looked like a member of the quinine and mineral water brigade.

Looking at the Noctis Shards, I realized how enigmatic they really were. Until found, and lost, by the French lunatic LaSalle, they were known only through the writings of Pliny (the Elder, not his social-climbing nephew), who gave them their name, and *he* only knew of them from certain Egyptian magical papyri now lost.

At one time, it must have been a single slab of dark stone, but was broke into shards, five of them. The obverses, facing upward in that cotton-filled tray were incised with images and proto-Egyptian inscriptions. Finally, I could see details omitted from the drawings, though, overall, they were surprisingly accurate.

"It tells of portals opened, of an ancient evil summoned from beneath what it calls 'a mountain of white water,' probably snow, I think, and the 'essence' of Atlach-Nacha," I said. "I now understand many things previous confusing, but overall …"

"Essence, you say?" Holmes asked.

"More or less." I looked at the word again. "Well, it could be interpreted as 'spoor' or 'spawn' as well. One is more a spiritual presence, the other more physical."

"Perhaps we are confronted by both," Holmes mused.

"How did you happen into this quagmire, Holmes?" I asked. "Ancient terrors, invasions of monster-gods, things that go squish in the night—a far cry from your usual bailiwick of blackmailers, murderers, and befuddled governesses."

"I was engaged to find Sir Walter Ferris," Holmes replied.

"I hired Mr Holmes, privately." Sir Charles stood about as far as he could from the Shards and still be in his office. He really was put off by them, the poor old duffer. "I was concerned about the provenance of the relics the moment they arrived from

Egypt. After all, artifacts lost in Cairo appearing in a tomb in Abydos is ..."

"Yes, yes," I murmured, examining the Shards with a glass sorry now I had asked. "Eminently understandable."

"I had planned to confront Professor Knight, but then there was his ... his unfortunate accident."

Unfortunate indeed! Especially for poor old Knight. I knew him slightly. Stuck me for a bar tab at the Diogenes Club. I could hardly shout at the villain as he ankled away without paying, not without incurring the wrath of Mycroft and other silent stuffed shirts.

"Sir Walter also returned to London, but he could not be found," Sir Charles continued. "I knew Holmes through ..."

"Yes, yes," I murmured. "Most interesting."

The Noctis Shards' story was more fascinating than anything Sir Charles could prattle on about. I was not at all surprised Holmes had found his way into my neck of the woods through entirely mundane means, a missing person. Despite the keenness of his intellect and his rigid unflappability (his oh-yes-I-knew-all-about-that attitude while the rest of us mortals stand about thoroughly gobsmacked), I had long suspected he not only accepted cases based on how interesting they were, but also on how completely they were grounded in the material world. No ghosts need apply, he told his Boswell after that sad kerfuffle in Sussex, but where was the Great Detective now? Chasing a giant spider. Or maybe being chased by one. Or pursuing something. Well, you know what I mean.

"If you will excuse me," Holmes said.

Sir Charles turned in alarm; I barely looked up.

"I must follow up on Sherrington's information," Holmes said. "I also need to utilize the museum's chemical laboratory."

Sir Charles protested vociferously. I was not sure if the old boy did not want to be left with the Noctis Shards, with me, or both. I had no idea what I had said to send Holmes scarpering, but damned if I was going to give him the satisfaction of asking. You know how he is—leaves us fumbling in the dark until he explains it all in the end and everything seems so painfully obvious and how could we all have possibly have missed it in the first place? No, not I.

Besides, I was turning over the Noctis Shards, revealing for the first time their long-hidden reverses. I sucked in a ragged breath.

"What?" Sir Charles turned from the closed door, but took not a step toward me. "What do you see?"

What I saw was startling, even to me, and it rather takes a lot to startle me, such as a giant snake in the sewers of Whitechapel, a demon bursting from the earth in Cornwall, or Aunt Dorcas unannounced at my door. Or, as in this case, inscriptions in a completely non-human language—the Elder Tongue.

When Cthulhu, Shub-Niggurath, Atlach-Nacha and the other Great Old Ones dropped in on Earth during antediluvian times, they brought their alien ways, including their own language. The alphabet used for the Elder Tongue is unearthly, created to express the concepts of minds not limited to our mundane views of time and space. Looking at the multi-dimensional symbols was enough to give one a sick headache. I was developing one.

Studying the Elder Tongue, even writing it, was one thing, but trying to actually give voice to the blasted thing was likely to shred your vocal cords, after which your brain would melt. Unless, of course, uttering the unutterable drove you stark barking mad first, *then* melted your brain. I imagine old Pharaoh Neferirkare had to pour his unlucky scribe into a sarcophagus after this particular job.

The inscription paralleled the tale told on the obverse, but in damnedable detail, blatantly exposing horrors only hinted at by the other scribe. It was not just the terrifying descriptions or names of monstrous entities dangerous to even mention, but the graphic images of creatures that should not have ever lived, but had. And still did. They seemed to move, to reach out for me, to call me ...

"Sherrington!"

My name echoed through the vastness of space, down the corridors of time. I wanted to look up, but the animate stone creatures on the Shards held me fast, wrapping about me sinuous arms, writhing tentacles and appendages with no earthly analogue. I felt as if I were being drawn into a gelatinous black mass, immobilizing and suffocating.

"Sherrington! For the love of God, man!"

With a supreme effort of will, I wrenched my gaze from images and words never meant for the mind of man. Sir Charles stared at me from the far corner of the room, pressed frantically against the joint of the walls. His eyes were wide, pupils mere pinpoints, and spittle dribbled from between clenched teeth. He was staring not at me, but past me. Abruptly, I realized my perusal of the Shards had not been a silent one. I had murmured the Elder Tongue!

Distant booms sounded, shotguns being discharged, I realized, but neither of us reacted to them. A dim light pulsed, separate from the lamplight. Thin shadows passed over Sir Charles's face. Suddenly, the old boy screamed, yanked open the door and scarpered as fast as a rat off a sinking ship. I was left alone in the office ... but I did not feel at all alone.

Shadows still shifted to and fro where Leigh had stood. Out the corners of my eyes I saw dark wands waving lazily about. An acrid smell assaulted me. At the same moment, I heard a hissing sigh, and a chill breath like a breeze from out of a slaughterhouse flowed over me. I did not want to turn about, see what fell terror had invaded our realm, but I knew I would. I had to. How could I not?

I thought I knew what I would see. I thought I was prepared for what I would find. I thought the unknown Egyptian scribe (poor damned soul) had caught the essence, the form and nature of that which he termed the 'spoor' of Atlach-Nacha. I was wrong, horribly and terribly wrong on all counts.

I saw a glittering blue phosphorescence hanging in the midst of the air. It crackled softly, as would an arc-lamp. Through the portal, I glimpsed a red-litten realm, a chamber in the volcanic depths through which huge spiders stalked on tree-trunk legs. In the scoriac light I spied hundreds of pale spheres similar to the one in the workroom where poor Oliphant was killed.

As startling as that vista was, however, it was a mere visual aside to that which captivated me, chilled me into immobility. A black form was crawling through that aperture, something very much like a spider with ropy, grasping tentacles. I gazed at it now halfway into our world, and *she* gazed back.

"Run, you fool!" a voice cried.

A huge hand grasped my shoulder and threw me back. The man was stout as a bull, black bearded, and wild-eyed. His coat was ragged and bloody, victim of at least one shotgun blast. I recognized him as Sir Walter Ferris.

"As foolish as Knight!" He now stood between me and the spoor of Atlach-Nacha. "He, too, opened the gateway. You've damned us all!"

I thought of protesting my innocence, but decided this was probably not the best of times to debate the matter. Besides, he had a point. Though I had not opened the portal purposely, it was indeed open.

"Run!"

I've often been called a fool, but no one has ever called me a coward. Perhaps one has something to do with the other. I should have run. That is something more obvious to me in retrospect than it was at the time. Instead of scarpering, I moved to where the injured Sir Walter, armed with only his gorilla-huge paws, had engaged the blasted creepy-crawly in mortal combat. I rushed forward to help before my fear could overwhelm my foolishness. What I received for my efforts was a swat from a truncheon-like appendage.

I landed by the desk, overturning the chair. Pulling myself up, I caught sight of the Shards. Since I had opened the portal to Hyperboria (inadvertently, mind you) with the Shards, perhaps I could close it as well.

Actually, I would much rather have faced that eight-legged, harpy-headed horror than look again upon the mind-destroying glyphs of the Elder Tongue. But, as the saying goes, "Cry havoc, and once more into the breach," or something like that.

The engraved monster-gods clutched at my senses and imagination. Savage pounding and guttural chants seemed to assault my ears, but I was in no state of mind to say whether they came from within or without. If the fragments possessed this much latent power, I could well understand why the tablet had been shattered.

I searched frantically for the incantation of dismissal. You see, it is one of the inviolable rules of magic that you never summon an otherworldly creature, be it demon, elemental, or snoozing Great Old One, without a way to send the blasted thing packing. I was betting that my unknown Egyptian scribe knew that as well.

And he did!

Muttering something under one's breath, unheard by even the speaker, is one thing, but quite another to give it full voice. It's the difference between peeping over a cliff and leaning into space. It's also the difference between sanity and going stark barking mad.

I don't remember—that's what I tell people, or at least those who haven't run for the hills by then. My throat felt as if I had quaffed a full jigger of acid. My tongue felt shredded and my eyes like bursting balls. It seemed as if my brain was flowing like melting candle wax, though some might claim that is business as usual for me, if you know what I mean.

Turning from the Shards to the lesser horror, I saw the portal collapse. By strength alone, Sir Walter had prevented the spoor from entering. Assorted legs and a head wearing a surprised expression clattered across the floor. I caught Sir Walter as he fell.

"Fools all of you," Sir Walter gasped. "I told Knight not to send the Shards here. Damned inscriptions! Thought he could control ..." He groaned and spasmed. The shotgun blasts from the guards had done him no good, but, even without them, his encounter with the spoor would have been deadly, poor blighter. "You must stop it."

I glanced at the dead thing. "Great Old One or not, there's no coming back from that."

He grabbed me by the lapels, drawing me close. "No! Not that! The egg! It's hatched, you fool. You must stop it before ... before it spawns ... spawns at ..."

Sir Walter was gone, but I now understood. Finally.

When he and Professor Knight entered the tomb in Abydos, they discovered the Noctis Shards. How did they get there? I can't know for certain, but I think Professor LaSalle transported them via an interdimensional portal, which he opened as I had opened one to Hyperboria, but on purpose, you understand. Also transported was an object LaSalle had found in the darkness of the Giza tomb, one he perhaps had not comprehended, a sphere composed of calcium and lime—an egg.

While poor Oliphant catalogued relics sent back from Egypt by the expedition, he probably ignored the sphere, mysterious and unfathomable. After a century in darkness it hatched. The spoor of Atlach-Nacha didn't kill him outright, giving him time to scratch a warning gleaned from whatever brief telepathic contact he had had. The meaning of Oliphant's message was now clear—at midnight the spoor of Atlach-Nacha would spawn a new generation, bringing apocalyptic destruction to London.

Foolish mortal. The accusation came not from Sir Walter but from the head of the creature I thought thoroughly dead. It blinked its molten eyes. *The Earth was ours and shall be again.*

Some semblance of life remained in that terrible head. I started to turn away, but found it much more satisfactory to boot it across the room. It was gone, its thoughts were out of my mind, and I felt much better, but for all too brief a moment as it turned out.

The door shattered and flew off its hinges. The eight-legged creature surging into the room was almost as big as what had tried to come through the portal, but its abdomen was swollen.

Legend had always held that the female head of Atlach-Nacha was extremely beautiful, lovely to behold and beguiling to the lonely. Well, so much for legend. She looked quite dodgy to me, and even worse when she saw what had befallen her sister. Her keening wail almost shattered my ears. I took advantage of her distraction and scarpered.

Like most men my age, I do try to take care of myself, even if I do drink too much, eat all the wrong foods, and spend the hours I should be asleep carousing, clubbing and fighting the forces of evil. Fueled by equal parts fear and adrenaline, I pounded down the corridor like sixty. Even so, I heard the pattering of the eight-legged beastie drawing ever closer.

The last thing Holmes said to me was something about using the museum's laboratory. I had no idea where it was, but I had to find it. Hysterical strength and obscure arcane knowledge are fine for most situations, but if I didn't want to end up like Oliphant or Sir Walter I needed Sherlock Holmes's intellect and resourcefulness.

I cried out, hoping Holmes would hear me. Or at least some blokes with shotguns would come running. What I had previously suspected about Atlach-Nacha had been confirmed by the fate of the spoor in Leigh's office. For all their mighty powers and extreme longevity, the Great Old Ones are yet as mortal as the least of us.

"Sherrington!" Holmes called. "This way, man!"

I ankled down a branching corridor, heading into deep shadows. Almost upon my heels, I heard the clattering and slithering of the spoor. I came to a steel-reinforced door. I ducked inside, pulling it after me.

Or rather, I attempted to close the door. Black ropy appendages curled around the edge and pulled. The door was yanked from my grasp. The spoor creature surged inside. I staggered back. The door slammed against the frame. The latching mechanism did not engage, but with that thing between me and the door, my ability to egress without dying was highly doubtful.

Pathetic mortal, you and the other naked apes are doomed. The voice echoed and churned in my mind. *After we take this land we shall summon our Mother, she who slumbers and dreams beneath the far mountain. She shall feast upon your kind.*

"Let sleeping spiders lie, I say."

A searing spike of hatred scorched its way through my brain. The psychic attack was accompanied by sanity-shattering fragments of the Elder Tongue, unencumbered by the inadequacies of human speech. From the long racial memory of the spoor of Atlach-Nacha I was assaulted by aeoned images of primal Earth, of the door to Saturn, and the livid realities of Cthulhu and the Great Old Ones moving among stars like drifting pollen. It was all a bit much, to tell you the truth, and I supposed I really did owe Holmes an apology for contesting the limits of my imagination.

Not that he would ever receive an apology, of course. Even were I to somehow avoid certain death, I was not about to give him the satisfaction of knowing he had been right about me. No need to feed the Great Detective's already-bursting ego, is there?

In amongst the terrible images force-fed me by Atlach-Nacha's spoor was one not from the Great Old Ones' salad years. This one was more in the nature of a prophecy— the metropolis aswarm with hundreds of little spoor, a vision of doomed London after midnight.

No wonder the old girl seemed swollen.

"I can't allow you to do this, madam." I don't know which startled me more, the calmness in my voice as I addressed her as I would an erring society matron or the way the Webley-Fosbery did not tremble one bit in my grip. "It would be very bad form were I to permit you to bring about London's destruction, a worldwide apocalypse, or anything of the sort. It just wouldn't be cricket."

I wasn't expecting an argument, but I had anticipated a leap or a pounce. At least a savage surge of fury that might leave my dismembered body bleeding heroically on the floor. Instead, the spoor's volcanic eyes locked me in a hateful stare, a Gorgon-like gaze from which I could not turn. Too late I recalled my own warning to Holmes about Atlach-Nacha's hypnotic abilities, augmented by her blistering telepathic talents.

Try as I might, I could not pull the trigger of my weapon. I told my muscles what to do, but they were out to lunch, so to speak.

You have no magicians to save you now, little ape, no Priests of Osiris to summon the destroying fire.

My throat was as frozen as my other muscles. At any time, it could have destroyed me, but it had not yet finished playing its cruel game of cobra to my wee little mousie.

Where we once failed in another city by a river, here we shall succeed. When I spawn my brood, it shall devour your kind, become heralds for the return of the Great Mother.

"Sorry, but I can't allow …" It hurt like the dickens to utter even those few words, but I could hardly let such impertinence go unanswered. I caught a flash of hot anger and felt a tightening of control, as if an octopus were squeezing my brain.

"Sherrington!"

Concurrent with Holmes's sharp call, the shadowy laboratory was flooded with brilliant flashes of light. They were, I understood immediately, tiny conflagrations of magnesium powder, a half-dozen of them in quick succession.

The brilliant bursts startled the spoor beast. More importantly, I felt her hold on me slip away. I emptied the Webley-Fosbery, the soft-nosed bullets slamming viscously into her bloated body. She fell to the ceramic floor, deflating rapidly.

You have not defeated me, pathetic ape!

Unfortunately, it wasn't spidery goo flowing out that made her deflate, but hundreds of her spawn, all pinkie-sized. Each of the little buggers (if I may so call them) had a head like its mum, and all looked as hungry as they did malevolent. And there I stood with an empty gun. Out of the frying pan and into the bleeding fire.

Then something grabbed my arm and I was propelled toward the door. Out the corner of my eye I caught Holmes's grim features and saw something bulky in his grasp. We flew out the laboratory. As we slammed the reinforced door into place, he threw his burden back inside.

"Holmes, what are you ..."

I once saw Holmes straighten out a bent fireplace poker, so I was surprised not to lose an arm when he yanked me to cover behind some stacked crates. Before I could protest further, an explosion within the laboratory deafened me and made the entire structure shudder. Then the steel door flew off its frame propelled by a searing tongue of flame.

When the flames subsided, I shook off Holmes and looked through the smoldering doorway. Nothing moved. I saw a blackened sea of crispy critters.

"Jolly good," I muttered.

I assume Holmes caught me as I fell.

I awoke in my Westminster Mansions flat, Giles above me spooning brandy down me. First thing I did after awakening was long-arm the bottle and administer myself a proper dose of brandy. Or two. Actually, it might have been three. After melting my brain by trying to speak an inhuman language and being accosted by a demented spider-monster in a family way, I felt I was entitled.

Giles withdrew, Holmes taking his place.

"I suppose it's after midnight?"

He nodded. "Long after midnight."

"No apocalypse?"

"London is as it always is."

"Well, I suppose nothing can be done about that." I looked askance at Holmes. "Are you waiting for me to thank you for saving my life? Well, you can keep waiting, boyo! If not for you, it would not have been endangered in the first place."

"And London might have been destroyed."

I frowned. "Well, there is that."

He patted my shoulder. "Everything worked out to the best, all thanks to you, my good fellow. London stands, the Empire endures, and the only casualties were James Oliphant and Sir Walter Ferris."

"And Professor Knight."

"Accidental death, according to Scotland Yard."

"What does your chum Lastrade have to say about Oliphant and Ferris?"

"Oliphant, apparently, contracted a deadly disease working with the artifacts from Egypt, and Sir Walter was accidentally shot by a guard," Holmes said. "Evidently, distraught by the death of Knight, he attempted to break into the Natural History Museum. A most unfortunate misunderstanding."

I smelled something rotten, and we were nowhere near Denmark. I also suspected the hand of that rascal Mycroft at play. Whenever Her Majesty's Government wants to bury something deep, Mycroft usually sends a minion with a spade to start digging.

"And the spoor of Atlach-Nacha?"

"The burned remains recovered from the museum's laboratory are inconclusive," Holmes replied. "Difficult to make anything of them."

I considered asking about the chopped-off fragments of the creature that tried to pass through the portal, but I had a sinking feeling where that line of enquiry would lead me. I entertained another sinking feeling (well, already sunk actually), but I had to ask anyway.

"The Noctis Shards are missing," Holmes replied.

Missing my left foot! Those relics were no more missing than any other object designated dangerous or embarrassing by the British government. No doubt the Shards were by now securely ensconced in some secret warehouse guarded by a cadre of agents, nestled amongst the original manuscript of the Necronomicon, spare parts for Martian war-machines, and perpetual motion devices.

"Don't take it so hard, Sherrington. It is for the best."

"What will others say when they discover what really happened at the Natural History Museum?" I demanded. "The government can hide the truth about the deaths, but not about the explosion."

"Gas leaks are very dangerous."

I sighed and flung myself against my pillow. "I guess no ghost *still* need apply at your agency. Is that it?"

Holmes nodded. "Officially."

"You and Mycroft and all his secret brethren can hoodwink the unwashed masses, but *I* know the truth."

"Yes, and if not for your insights into the creature's mortality, as well as its telepathic and spawning capabilities, a solution to the emergency would not have presented itself to me."

"You're not the first, you know, Holmes." His expression did not change, but it seemed to me his thin lips tightened a bit. "The reverse of the Noctis Shards revealed that Pharaoh Neferirkare's chestnuts were pulled out of the fire, so to speak, by the Priests of Osiris. To route the invasion of the spoor and destroy the seething spawn they used what they called the Breath of Ra, something like Greek Fire." I paused. "Perhaps not unlike that incendiary device you tossed in as we scarpered out."

I don't know what I was hoping for. If I had thought to knock Holmes down a peg or two by revealing that those ancient johnnies had been just as resourceful as he, I might have saved my breath to cool my porridge. The tightness of his lips never actually resolved itself into a grimace of dismay. Drat!

"I understand you'll be up and around in a day or two." He looked to Giles. "Try to keep him on a short leash."

"I'll do my best, Sir."

"No one is going to tell me what to do."

"I could ask one of your aunts to look after you, sir."

"Very well," I grumbled. "I'll be good."

"I'll take my leave now, knowing you are in good hands." Holmes started out the door, then looked back. "I'm sure you'll be fit as a fiddle by ... say, Friday next?"

Then he was gone, a smirky smile upon his lips—the cad.

POSITIVE DENIAL

A You-Solve-It By Laird Long

Sir Loch Hoames and his new bride, Dr. Watt-Sun, were taking a tour of the Ozark County Courthouse when Sheriff Les Tradd gestured at the honeymooning couple from a small room adjoining an interrogation cell.

"Glad you're here, Sir Loch!" Sheriff Tradd gasped, as the recently married pair entered the room and looked through the one-way glass at a man sitting calmly at a wooden table inside the cell next door.

"I've been questioning Professor Maury R. Tee for over an hour, but I just can't get him to crack. We're sure he's the guilty party in the 'backwoods bookworm' murder case. Would you mind having a go at him?"

Hoames, of course, leapt at the opportunity like a hound at a Baskerville. He'd read all about the celebrated cerebral country case in the local newspapers. And *anything* to postpone another Branson religious revival theater show with his beloved betrothed.

Amongst his many other talents, the amateur sleuth had a well-known knack for breaking down recalcitrant suspects, playing on their personal weaknesses, fears and foibles until they burst out with the truth. But the number one suspect in the murder of Camille Tee appeared as cool as the weather outside wasn't, smiling at the two men and one woman behind the glass.

Professor Maury R. Tee's wife had been found bludgeoned to death in the study of bibliophile Sam Struthers's house, a large Oxford English dictionary (v.06) lying next to her body. Struthers had been outside in the garage at the time of the murder, so he said, had discovered the body and called the police.

The professor admitted knowing that his wife was cheating on him with Struthers, but claimed he didn't care. He seemed more concerned about the other man beating him to publication of a complete bibliography of long-dead literary writer Caresse Keller.

The tall, bespectacled murder suspect was an English instructor at College of the Ozarks, a well-respected coach of the school debate and poetry slam teams. As Sheriff

Tradd now informed Sir Loch, the professor was nicknamed 'Word' by his students, because of his uncompromising respect for the English language, a reputation as a strict grammarian with a severe predilection for punctuation.

"Indeed!" Sir Loch exclaimed with glee, being rather punctilious himself, as well as a fine dialect mimic. "Allow me to break him down for you!"

The lean sleuth stormed into the interrogation cell and smacked his slender hands down onto the table in front of Tee, pushing his angular face up close. "We ain't gettin' nowheres here, T!" he bellowed. "Where was you 'tween nine and ten a' clock last night?"

The suspected spouse slayer flinched. "The correct sobriquet is Mr. *Tee*, or Professor Tee. Perhaps you should attend one of my classes. It might—"

"Don't lecture me none, T-each! Just youse answer the question, 'kay."

Professor Tee said, "I was at home revising a paper on the grammatical origins of 'farther' and 'further', when—"

"Nobody seen ya, right?"

"As I told the sheriff, I was alone at—"

"While your wife were makin' it with Sam Struthers!"

Tee's face reddened. "Apparently."

"You coulda murdered da bum for that, huh?"

"Hardly. Camille and I had not—"

"An' what about that there bibio thing-a-majigger? That's 'nother thing he stole off'n you, huh?"

"Really! I do not see any—"

"Anyways, you hated the guy's guts. You ain't foolin' me none, T."

The professor gritted his teeth. "Sir, your English is—"

"Don't speak good nuff for youse, huh? Ir-re-gardless, that don't matter. What matters are you was mad enough to kill your Missus—could of and did!"

The corners of Maury R. Tee's mouth twitched, his burning face streaked with the hot spittle of Hoames's mangled syntax. "I have nothing more to—"

"Yawl talk, Mr. T! T'ain't never been the man born I ain't done being able to break down!"

"Sir, your language is atrocious!" Professor Tee screamed.

"You tellin' me you didn't not murder your wife!?" Sir Loch roared back.

"That is correct!"

Hoames smacked the table again, the two men glaring at one another inches apart.

Then the great detective straightened his lanky frame and stalked out of the interrogation cell and into the adjoining room.

"Well, you gave it a good try," Sheriff Les Tradd sighed.

Hoames grinned. "I certainly think so."

Tradd's expression went from disappointment to astonishment, when the visiting sleuth added, "Book Professor Maury R. Tee for the murder of his wife, Camille Tee. And make sure you 'read' him his rights, in clear English."

Solution in next month's issue ...

THE HALLOWEEN BANDIT

A You-Solve-It By James Glass

It was lunchtime at Pleasant Grove Elementary. Johnny Copper looked for a place to sit. The cafeteria was crowded with kids eating and talking about what they wanted to be that night. Some even wore their costumes to school, but not Johnny. He would wait until it got dark outside before getting dressed up as his favorite sleuth, Sherlock Holmes. He found an open seat and set his tray on the table.

"I'm having a Halloween party at my house tonight. Do you want to come?" Griffin Peterson asked. "My parents are setting up a haunted house in the garage. It will be very scary, I assure you. My dad told me to invite some friends to be the first to enter."

Johnny opened his carton of milk and took a sip. "How many kids are coming?"

Griffin started counting his fingers. "Ten ... I think. Be at my house at 7:00 P. M. That's when it's supposed to be ready."

Johnny ate a piece of meatloaf. It tasted like burnt cardboard. He took a sip of milk to swallow the horrible taste.

"That would be great," Johnny said.

After dinner, Johnny went to his bedroom and put on his costume. He looked at himself in the mirror on the back of his door. The deerstalker hat, which resembled a black top hat, completed the ensemble.

He picked up his flashlight and walked out the front door.

The night sky seemed to morph into another world as the moon disappeared behind gray clouds. The wind howled like an angry scream. Many of the kids carried glow sticks.

Johnny turned on his flashlight and began trick or treating. By the time he finished, he had been to more houses and collected more goodies than any other Halloween he thought.

As he walked toward Griffin's house, his candy bucket started to get heavy. When his arm began to ache from the weight of the candy, he switched hands.

When Johnny reached the house, he saw a giant purple inflatable spider in the front yard. Next to it was a graveyard with tombstones. One read, 'Here lays our son, Ted, Once alive but now is dead.' Another read, 'Eeny meeny miny moe, Jeremiah died when he stubbed his big toe.'

Then Johnny noticed a vampire next to the porch. At first, he thought it was part of the decorations, but then he saw the bloodsucker working on a bike. It was Craig Billings.

"My chain came loose," Craig said. The boy connected it around the sprocket, turned the pedal and the chain worked its way back on.

Craig stood, grabbed a pillowcase filled with candy, walked up the steps, and stood next to the junior detective at the front door. They could hear eerie music coming from the garage. Johnny knocked on the door and the two boys waited.

A boy dressed as a ghost walked up the steps and stood behind Johnny and Craig.

"Boo," the boy said.

"Who are you?" Craig asked.

"It's me. Joshua Bennett."

"Well, you're not scary."

Johnny laughed. Joshua didn't.

The door opened and a tall man dressed as Frankenstein stood at the door.

"Hello," the man said in a deep voice. "Enter at your own risk." He let out a boisterous laugh.

It startled all three boys and they each took a step back.

Frankenstein smiled. "Don't worry. It's just me, Mr. Peterson."

When they entered the house, Johnny saw seven other boys, including Griffin sitting in the living room eating candy from their buckets, except for Bobby Reynolds, dressed as Captain America—he watched *It's The Great Pumpkin, Charlie Brown* special on the television.

"Okay, kids. The haunted house is ready," Frankenstein said. "Put your candy away for now. You can pick it up when you go home."

"Let's put it in the kitchen," Griffin said. He was dressed as a werewolf.

All the kids set their candy on the table and followed Mr. Peterson to the door leading out to the garage.

When the kids entered the garage, a skeleton dropped down from overhead. Everyone screamed. Craig ran back into the house. As the kids stepped further into the haunted house, white smog began to cover the floor. Johnny wondered what scary thing might pop out next: spiders, witches, or maybe even an axe murderer. He jumped as someone grabbed his arm. He turned and saw Craig had returned. The music seemed to be getting louder. Then a woman screamed. All the kids jumped.

Griffin who was leading the pack, stopped.

"Let's keep going," Craig said.

"I don't know if I want to go any further," Joshua said. "Maybe we should turn back."

A flash of light came from the ceiling followed by the sound of thunder. The kids didn't move.

"It's just a haunted house," Craig said. "Nothing here can hurt you."

Johnny noticed Craig had found his courage since rejoining the group. The junior detective felt a little sick to his stomach. He tried to swallow, but his mouth was dry.

"Just follow me," Craig said and moved up to the front of the line.

As the boys followed Craig through the gauntlet of surprises, a ghost flew over their heads and they ducked, disappearing into the white fog. They crawled next to a coffin leaning against the wall. It flew open and a zombie reached out to them. The kids screamed again, stood and raced to the back door. A bloody hand appeared from the depths of the mist, the fingers moved like a spider, and reached for them. Each kid avoided its grasp and ran outside into the yard.

"That was fun," Craig said. "Let's do it again."

Some of the kids laughed.

"Not me," Joshua said. "I'm going home."

Everyone except Joshua went through the haunted house again.

Johnny realized it wasn't as scary the second time around. When everyone got back into the house, Griffin said, "Someone stole our candy."

Craig said, "Joshua's not here. He must have taken it before he went home."

"If Joshua's not here," one of the other boys said, "he must have taken the candy. There's no other explanation."

A few of the kids nodded in agreement.

Johnny counted nine empty buckets. The pillowcase was missing. Maybe Joshua did steal the candy, he thought. Then he noticed black finger smudges on the outside edge of each bucket. "No," he said. "Whoever stole the candy is still here. And I know who it is?"

Did you solve the case too?

Solution in next month's issue ...

SOLUTION TO SEPTEMBER'S YOU-SOLVE-IT

Egg On His Face By Laird Long

"Lynn and Stu are out because they were out in the field with me, beating the bushes for painted eggs. Beryl and Jim were inside the building, but they had no way of knowing you weren't still locked in my office with your egg—nobody saw you leave."

I hopped to a conclusion, "But *Hazel* saw you go into the men's washroom, so she knew you'd left my office unguarded, could glom the golden egg for herself before all the painted ones were counted."

73147285R00071

Made in the USA
San Bernardino, CA
01 April 2018